Guns of Vengeance

Jackson Cole

WHEELER
CHIVERS

This Large Print edition is published by Wheeler Publishing,
Waterville, Maine USA and by BBC Audiobooks Ltd,
Bath, England.

Published in 2006 in the U.S. by arrangement with
Golden West Literary Agency.

Published in 2006 in the U.K. by arrangement with
Golden West Literary Agency.

U.S. Softcover   1-59722-280-1   (Western)
U.K. Hardcover 10: 1 4056 3868 0   Chivers Large Print)
U.K. Hardcover 13: 978 1 405 63868 5
U.K. Softcover 10: 1 4056 3869 9   (Camden Large Print)
U.K. Softcover 13: 978 1 405 63869 2

The text of this Large Print edition is unabridged.
Other aspects of the book may vary from the original edition.

Set in 16 pt. Plantin by Carleen Stearns.

Printed in the United States on permanent paper.

British Library Cataloguing-in-Publication Data available

Library of Congress Cataloging-in-Publication Data

Cole, Jackson.
    Guns of vengeance / by Jackson Cole.
      p. cm. — (Wheeler Publishing large print westerns)
    ISBN 1-59722-280-1 (lg. print : sc : alk. paper)
    1. Large type books. I. Title. II. Series: Wheeler large print
western series
PS3505.O2685G865 2006
813'.52—dc22   2006010189

Guns of Vengeance

Guns of Vengeance

When settlers west of the Pecos are the prey of scheming rustlers and land-grabbers, the Lone Wolf Ranger comes a-riding to deliver justice with a pair of smoking guns!

Chapter I

Savage Range

Hal Lewiston, a cowman who had but recently settled in west Texas gave a contented sigh as he paused to rest in his sweated saddle. Looking over the central Pecos range, he watched a party of riders coming north toward him on a trail bordering the winding river canyon, and waited, idly wondering about them.

It was a wild, striking country, where the black-watered mighty Pecos cut Texas. Men had to work hard here to win a bare subsistence from the semi-arid earth. The Trans-Pecos stretched west, a great plateau covered by sparse bunch grasses and prickly pear, and split by deep canyons at the bottom of which the streams ran, refusing their moisture to the land.

Yet here was an oasis, too, one section where a retaining dam controlled the discharge of great springs. The grass was actually greener and more animals could graze and grow sleek and fat.

It was new, new with promise, and that was what Lewiston liked. Hope was what men live by and Hal Lewiston, a big, dark-haired man of around forty had the eagerness of a much younger man. Starting with a small herd of cattle, he expected to build it up until he was well-off, and could give his wife and children everything they had ever desired. There were about ten men in the party which came over to meet him where he sat his horse, waiting.

"Howdy, boys," he greeted heartily, for he was a man of naturally generous manner.

"Ugh."

The long-legged, powerful man in the van grunted crossly, like an Indian, as he pulled his powerful stallion to a stop and regarded the rancher with eyes as bright as emeralds. He wore scratched leather — chaps and a flapping jacket. At his waist were black-stocked six-shooters and his manner was so hostile that Lewiston began to feel vaguely ill-at-ease.

Under the curved dark Stetson the rider

showed matted hair the color of new bricks. His snub nose twitched a bit, over his crisp reddish mustache. One great hand on which the knuckles stood out white against the bronzed skin, gripped the stallion's reins. The red-haired man's other hand rested at his jutting hip, the arms akimbo. He had bony, wide shoulders. In fact, all his joints protruded, for he was as raw-boned as a starved steer.

The men with him were of like stamp, though not so pronounced. Four wore Mexican getups — steeple sombreros, tight-fitting pants and short jackets — and were dark of hide, glinting of eye. The rest were men from the American side of the Border, hard-faced and wearing leather or other material capable of resisting the thorns of the chaparral. All were heavily armed, not only with two Colts apiece, but with shotguns or carbines in special saddle sockets.

"My handle's Lewiston, gents," said the cowman, to break the strain he was under at that cold stare. "I'm runnin' a herd here."

The emerald eyes flicked to the score or so of cows which Lewiston had just run into a grassy hollow to graze.

"Ugh," the leader of the strange riders

repeated, then he spoke, his voice rasping like a dull saw in tough wood. "So I see, so I see. You want to know my handle? I'm Pecos Carns." As Lewiston showed no nervousness or fear as the name was mentioned, he added, "King of the Rustlers, they call me."

"Yeah?" said Lewiston, grinning. He knew there were plenty of tough characters in west Texas. But he wasn't looking for trouble.

"Yeah," said Pecos Carns. "Been down in Mexico courtin' for a spell. How long you figger on stayin' in these parts, mister?"

"Oh, permanent-like," Lewiston said easily. "Got a house and corrals a-buildin' over the hill."

"Ugh. That all the cattle yuh run?"

"Nope. I got about two hundred breeders to start. 'Course the others got more — like John Fenton and the rest."

"What others?"

"Why, my friends that came into this section with me. We're settlin' here, Carns, filed on the land legal-like. Got a little town — Fentonville she's called — near the dam yuh see there."

Pecos Carns suddenly exploded in rage. "Every one of yuh'll get!" he declared.

"This is my range, savvy? You cussed squatters are a nuisance, bringin' in folks and the Law. I don't want yuh round here!"

"But Silas Barstowe, the banker, fixed it all up!" protested Lewiston. "You must be wrong. This land ain't been proved up before we come, Carns. Yuh'll have to take it up with Barstowe and Fenton."

"I'm takin' it up with you, here and now," snarled Carns. "Joe, you and Mike drive them cows over to the place. We'll need meat for supper."

"Wait a jiffy!" snapped Lewiston. "Those are my cows!"

His hand moved, upward, really in a gesture of objection. But Pecos Carns hardly needed any excuse. The black-stocked Colt by his right hand flew out and up, exploding, and Hal Lewiston's dreams ended with a bullet to the heart.

Carns' red mustache flicked as he watched Lewiston quiver his last on the ground.

"Cussed squatters," he repeated. "They'll wreck our hide-out. It's too good a set-up to quit."

"How about the rest of 'em, and their town, Pecos?" asked the man he had called Joe.

"I'll clean 'em out."

11

"Do we throw this hombre in the river?"

"Naw, leave him. The buzzards got to eat."

Pecos Carns and his men rode off, the cattle moving ahead of them.

Young Nat Fenton swung off his chestnut mustang with a trained rider's ease, dropping the reins over the hitch-rack near the main structure in the new town of Fentonville. It was a square wooden edifice marked by a sign in printed red letters which said:

CENTRAL PECOS DEVELOPMENT CO.

Fenton's blue eyes shone with pleasure and pride as he looked up at this. His father's name was printed there in letters only a bit smaller than the designation. "John Fenton — Pres."

At the right of the company's office was that of Silas Barstowe, the investment banker who had sparked the new settlement.

Nat Fenton was a slim but well-knit young fellow, all muscle and sinew, like the wiry mustangs he loved to catch and ride. He was an outdoors man to whom this land was a boon. Hunting, dangerous work with wild horses and cattle, scouting, Indian fighting — all appealed to him. He was fitted for such a life, too, for he had never known a moment's illness, and much preferred to sleep under the open sky than inside a stuffy building.

He wore soft buckskin garments, oiled half-boots, and a sand-hued Stetson was cocked on his crisp brown hair. His pleasant, eager, sun-bronzed young face was clean-shaven, a face that showed Nat Fenton loved the life he lived. His smile came easily, to add to that impression, as he surveyed the new town.

As yet there were but a dozen structures in Fenton, set back from the Pecos canyon on the western side of the stream. In the elevations nearby, giant springs had been discovered and dug out, and a dam had been built. When the springs had been cleaned, their flow proved large enough to supply not only the settlement but the small ranches whose owners had been brought in by the Company in order to prove the new sections.

It was an unusual spot, an oasis in the generally dry Trans-Pecos. For ages the land had lain unused by man, crossed only by animals, and now and then by the red savages who paused by the springs to drink. That land had been as worthless as gold which lies hidden in the ground, where, no one knows. Unless men wanted the land it was of no more account than the hidden metal.

But now men had come to live upon it, to raise their food there, and so it assumed its proper place. It was already growing in price, since it was desired.

Down the single reddish-dirt street stood a small saloon, the "Pecos Inn." There whisky, and sometimes beer were sold. It was a meeting place for men who came to town. There was also a general store in town, but as yet it carried only a few supplies — flour, hardtack, canned beans, shovels, some bolts of cloth, and sunbonnets. Now and then a load of potatoes came in by wagon and were quickly bought up. The store also had ammunition in stock for the hunting rifles and Colts of the settlers.

Yet the settlement was complete, even to a town loafer, a good-natured drunkard everyone called "Old Pete," who had drifted in from nowhere the day the saloon opened. Old Pete bobbed up before Nat now, grinning.

"Howdy, boy," he greeted. "Mighty dry day, ain't it?"

Pete wore the same tattered hand-medowns, and the felt hat with holes in the crown that he had worn on the day he hit town. Old Pete claimed those holes were made by a bullet passing clean through his hat. He would always tell a story for whisky, though since his tales differed each time, he was looked upon simply as a source of amusement. He was a vague old fellow whose black whiskers were salted with gray, and whose grin was permanent.

"Yeah, fearful dry, Pete," young Fenton agreed. "Here, have one on me." He handed Old Pete a four-bit piece, and the man reached the bar with businesslike alacrity.

Nat saw a small wagon up the street in front of the general store, so he chose to go there instead of to the Pecos Inn. He knew that rig, and was highly pleased when he found Emily Tate inside the emporium, as he had hoped. The smile of yellow-haired Emily, the eighteen-year-old daughter of George Tate, a Pecos settler, always stirred Nat Fenton to the heart.

"Howdy, Em!" Nat called as he saw her, a girl who looked fragile, but who was strong and lithe, for Emily Tate had pioneer blood.

"Nat!" she cried happily, smiling up at him. "Where have you been? We've missed you."

"I've been huntin' on the other side of the Peaks," he told her. "Had good enough luck. . . . Everybody well and happy?"

"Father's pleased, and we're all well, far as our family goes," said Emily.

Nat bought the girl some rock candy he saw on a store shelf, and a blue ribbon. Then he strolled up the road with Emily to have a good talk.

"I suppose you heard of Hal Lewiston's killing, Nat?" Emily asked.

"No!" He was shocked. "What happened?"

"They found him shot through the heart, lying not far from the river canyon, Nat," Emily said soberly. "Some of his cows were gone. There was a trail showing that ten men had met him, shot him, and driven off the cattle. The folks here believe rustlers did it, but the men who searched lost the sign a few miles northwest, in a maze of ravines and bush."

"I'm mighty sorry," Nat said gravely. "I'd shore like to come up with them killers."

"You be careful, won't you, Nat?" Emily's big brown eyes were anxious, and there was anxiety in her voice. She knew Nat Fenton, and to what lengths he might go, seeking revenge. "They're dangerous men."

Fenton nodded, but he was thinking of the murdered rancher. Hal Lewiston had been a good friend of Nat's father. He had come here to west Texas because of John Fenton.

Nat and Emily were near the new land office, when they saw a buggy approaching, coming in from the south along the river trail.

"Here comes Si Barstowe," remarked Nat. "Does he know about Lewiston and the rustlers?"

Emily nodded. "Yes. Though he's been away for a while now, on important business, I heard. He's such a fine man, Nat, isn't he?"

"Yeah, he shore is," Nat agreed. "Set us all up here all right."

As the buggy neared, John Fenton emerged from the land office door. Nat's father was a man nearing fifty, a solid, steady fellow with earnest eyes, and whose brown hair was graying at the temples. He was heavier than his son, but they had a close family resemblance. It was plain that John had looked much like his elder son when he had been Nat's age.

"Nat, my boy!" he cried, and gripped his son's hand. "Glad you're back!"

Chapter II

The Pussyfooter

Fenton's ranch lay a few miles west of the settlement. There lived John Fenton, his wife, and his daughter Sue, and Jack, Jr., who was two years younger than Nat.

The house was built of native timber and brush. Water was brought to it through a wooden conduit, and three hundred cows had been turned loose on the new range, to increase throughout the coming years into a herd.

There was not much work yet on the little spread. Young Jack took care of the chores, and the father, John Fenton, had a good deal of administrative work to do in connection with the Central Pecos Development Company.

Nat was aware of what a hard struggle his father had had to earn a living and bring up his family. The elder Fenton had been a small rancher on the Colorado, but had been shoved out there by big interests who had taken over the range. He had come to the Pecos for a new start in life, and all he desired now was to make good for the sake of his sons and his daughter.

Respected and loved for his honesty and for his kindly, even disposition, John Fenton had drawn others of his kind to him. They had followed him here, to settle the range, to work hard in building their herds, and in raising their families.

They were not wealthy people, but men who had scraped and saved a bit on which to begin new lives in a new land. They loved the land, were hungry for it. It was life to them, for on it their animals subsisted, and crops would grow to feed them all. These small investors, men such as Fenton and Tate, had put all they had into the Central Pecos Development Company.

The buggy Nat and Emily had seen approaching came to a stop, the sweated horse lowering his head after the pull uphill. A large man got down, smiling at the young people and at John Fenton, giving all three a hearty, voluble greeting.

His head was big, his hair dark and thick. He had a broad nose and gleaming teeth, and sideburns adorned his fat pink cheeks. His black frock coat, and the trousers tucked into soft leather elastic-sided shoes were expensive, and the soft, warm

19

air wafted from him a faint odor of per-fumed hair tonic and the aromatic smoke from a Cuban cheroot that he held in a well-fleshed hand. A thick gold watch-chain depended from pocket to pocket across his portly stomach, a bear tooth mounted in yellow metal hanging as a fob.

Silas Barstowe was a man whose entire appearance exuded respectability. There was also benevolence in his bearing, and in the deep voice in which he greeted his ad-miring friends.

"Have a good trip, Mr. Barstowe?" in-quired John Fenton, shaking the banker's hand.

"Very good, very good indeed, thank you," boomed Barstowe. "Nat, my boy, how are you this beautiful afternoon? And pretty Em? Always a pleasure to look at you, my dear."

Nat grinned, and Emily flushed and smiled at the compliment as Barstowe pinched her cheek in a fatherly manner. To them Silas Barstowe was a great man, the one man who had made this development possible, and given them a chance to own their lands and homes.

He was so kind, so good. He had lent sums of money with which to buy tools and seed and other necessities. To them he was a benefactor who had magically appeared to help them. And it seemed that his only interest was altruistic, though he could afford it. For they all knew, from hints dropped, that Barstowe had large interests in the East.

Barstowe and Nat's father went into the banker's spacious office. Emily and Nat finished their walk and returned to the girl's wagon. She had to be home in time to help with the evening meal and other chores, and Nat rode his chestnut mustang alongside the vehicle, talking with her on the way to her home.

The Tate place was only a few miles from the new settlement. As was the case at the Fenton ranch, the house was supplied with water which flowed from a spring through a wooden pipe into an earthen tank. There was water in plenty for family use and for the stock. Tate had some breeders on the range.

A two-room cabin had already been built, and Tate was well along with his work of erecting a barn and corrals. The ranch, which he called the Square T, stood on a flat expanse, with rising terrain to the west and north. Eastward lay the tortuous canyon of the Pecos.

Today, Tate was working on a lean-to at

the rear of the house, and Emily's sixteen-year-old brother Sam was helping him. George Tate was the picture of a man working hard for his family, in his blue overalls with the pockets sagging with nails and tools.

His heavy body bulged the faded overalls, and both his light, curly hair and his mustache needed trimming.

He did not bother to stop his work as his daughter drove up, with Nat Fenton riding his horse beside her. Tate merely nodded. He liked young Fenton all right, but hardly liked the idea of regarding him as Emily's suitor. Tate believed that his daughter was still too young to marry and leave home for one of her own.

But Emily's brother had a greeting for Nat.

"Hullo, yuh old rascal!" Sam called flippantly, winking at Nat.

Nat called back a cheery greeting, then carried the flour and the other supplies into the house. Em's mother kissed him, and insisted he stay for supper.

Nat Fenton ate with the Tates, and slept in the unfinished barn that night, but his plans were all made before his eyes closed. By dawn, he had saddled up and was on his way. The excitement of the chase was on him, and this time he wouldn't be tracking animals, but men, far more dangerous than the bears and other game he was accustomed to stalk. The night before he had learned all there was to know of Lewiston's death, where the body had been found and so on. Now he was determined to track down the rancher's killers.

The sun was reddening the sky as he hunted over the ground near the Pecos trail where Lewiston had died some days before. The sign was cold now, of course, and had been trampled over by less skillful investigators. But still Nat Fenton found enough to set him on the trail.

It led him northwest, but after a few miles the country grew so thick with thorned brush, and there were so many branching ravines, that he felt it was hopeless to go on. He climbed to a high spot and made himself comfortable. If he watched long enough, something might develop.

The sun had come to its noon zenith and declined, and it was around three in the afternoon when Nat Fenton saw a horseman emerge from an apparently impenetrable thorned thicket. He was followed by others, and Fenton watched them with deep interest.

The leader, a raw-boned fellow with carrot-hued hair, had a tough aspect, as did his heavily armed followers. The sun shone on rifle barrel and Colt steel, and Nat had a hunch he had not waited in vain.

There were fifteen men in the party. They headed toward Fentonville and Nat began to trail them. A mile out from town they stopped and hid until dark. Nat, keeping in hiding himself, had some trouble keeping track of them but when the moon came up he drew closer, and was not far behind when they entered the settlement.

There was a lamp burning in Barstowe's office, and the stealthy rustlers crept to the place. Young Fenton slid around behind the building, in the dark, and found a rear window, partially open.

The big, brick-haired man who was the leader of the tough riders that Fenton had been following stood in the center of the office, facing Silas Barstowe who sat rigid behind his flat-topped desk. It was a well-furnished office, with a carpet and comfortable chairs, and on the walls were several framed mottoes of upright sentiments. One that Nat could read proclaimed "Do Unto Others As You Would Have Others

Do Unto You." Another adjured, "Honesty Is The Best Policy," and still another reminded that "All That Glitters Is Not Gold."

Close behind Barstowe stood a cabinet containing decanters of liquor and boxes of cigars. A small stack of papers was on the desk near his hand, and a big file was against the wall.

The carrot-topped tough was angry. His voice rasped as he reviled Barstowe, Fentonville's benefactor, and every word was plain to the listening Nat. Several of the other riders were disposed in belligerent attitudes about the room.

"You cussed old pussyfooter!" accused Carrot-top, shaking his Colt at Barstowe. "You chase these fool squatters out of here or I'll make a sieve of yuh! Yuh're wreckin' my business. This section's my stampin' grounds, and yuh know me! I'm Pecos Carns, King of the Rustlers!"

Carns, apparently, was proud of his reputation as a bad man.

Nat Fenton, crouched right under the window, had a Colt drawn. There were eight of the chief rustler's cronies inside. Nat wondered where the rest were, but dared not desert his post for fear that Carns would fire on Barstowe.

Barstowe laughed. "Sit down, Mr. Carns, sit down. Please have a drink. I'm not armed, so you can put up the gun. Here, try some of this fine old Napoleon brandy. I reserve it for special occasions."

Nat admired Barstowe's nerve, faced by such fierce outlaws as Pecos Carns and his cattle thieves. He pushed against the house wall, silent in the dark, waiting to come to Barstowe's aid, if necessary.

Barstowe turned slowly and took a decanter with a red diamond-shaped label on it from the cabinet, which he had unlocked. He poured a stiff drink of the rich golden brandy for Carns, smiling benevolently at the red-headed man. Carns blinked, but sniffed and accepted the glass. He raised it to his lips, to swallow it in a gulp, but Barstowe stopped him.

"Don't do it, son," the banker said sharply. "It's loaded with strychnine. Enough poison in that to kill a grizzly bear and ten of you besides!"

Pecos Carns jumped two inches off the floor.

"Why, yuh cussed old lobo!" he gasped.

"I only wished to prove to you I'm not as helpless as I look," said Barstowe, pleased with the impression he had made. "Or as easy. I could have killed you but I didn't.

And I can use you. We'll work together."

Barstowe chose another flask. This time he poured a drink first for himself and downed it, before he pushed it to Carns.

"Drink up, boys," he ordered. "This is the stuff."

If Pecos Carns was astonished, Nat Fenton was struck dumb. All power had left his limbs. He could scarcely believe what his brain recorded.

"These people you wish to drive away, Carns," began Barstowe, "make the land valuable. It's worth a fortune simply because it's proved. The Development Company has lent them money so they may further improve the properties."

"I don't savvy," Carns said gruffly. "You set 'em up. They start herds, and increase 'em. Then they sell some, pay yuh up, and they're clear. What's in it for me, or even for you?"

Barstowe's smile was patient. He was like a professor listening to the sophomoric questions of a student.

"Why don't you leave these details to me, Carns?" he suggested. "I have had a great deal of experience in such deals. It's all legal, to the last scratch of the pen. I will tell you this much. These ranches have been started, and there are always other men waiting with cash to buy such places. The main dependence of the cowmen here is on their cattle herds. Suppose someone runs off these animals and the owners are unable to meet their obligations?"

Pecos Carns was fascinated. "Why, yuh sly old rascal!" he exclaimed admiringly, as the scheme penetrated his consciousness. "It looks like there's a million in it."

"There is." Barstowe nodded. "But I need you. I've been watching for just this connection, Carns. What do you say? It'll be fifty-fifty, but you must pay your men out of your share."

"It's a deal," Carns said promptly. "Sounds like a gold mine."

"You'll run off each brand of cattle as I tell you to," continued Barstowe. "I'll start with the Square T. That's George Tate. You're welcome to sell the cows in Mexico or elsewhere. And I'll dispose of the real estate."

Nat Fenton's heart was icy. He felt weak as he heard Silas Barstowe expose himself as a deadly opportunist who had used John Fenton to draw in the victims who were to be fleeced. Details were not all clear to Nat, but he had heard enough.

So stunned was he that at first he failed to catch the soft tread of a man turning the back corner. When he did hear he tried to whirl, to get up his Colt, but there were two more right behind the first, and they saw his head against the yellow shaft of light from the window.

They were quick to fall upon him, and a shotgun barrel half-stunned Nat as it slashed on his head.

They dragged him inside, and held him up before Barstowe and Pecos Carns.

"Why, this is Nat Fenton!" exclaimed Barstowe. There was no smile on his face now. Instead, it was grim.

"He was listenin' outside the back winder!" growled one of Nat's captors.

"I didn't hear anything, Mr. Barstowe," Nat lied. "I just seen yore light and so I come over to see if yuh was all right — and these hombres jumped me."

"I see."

Barstowe turned in his chair. He picked up the decanter with the red diamond label, poured a drink and held it out to Nat across the desk.

"You look shaky, my boy," he said calmly. "Here, drink this down."

Nat Fenton shook his head. He would not drink the poisoned liquor.

"He's heard everything!" cried Barstowe.

Pecos Carns cursed. The King of the

Rustlers jumped on Nat, whose arms were held. Carns' lips had a cruel twist as he punched Nat in the body. As Nat doubled up, Carns hit him in the face, smashing his lip into his teeth.

Nat tried to fight but men were all about him. He went down under the weight of their punches, and Pecos Carns, swearing a blue streak, began kicking him in the head and face with his sharp-toed, spurred boots. He kicked again and again with all the power of his strong body behind it, until Nat Fenton lay quivering, his head and face a bloody mess.

Barstowe watched, his expression unchanging until they had finished with Nat.

"Take it out of here, Carns," the banker said then, "and when you call on me again be more circumspect. Our connection must not be suspected."

Chapter III

The Long Arm of the Law

Captain William McDowell stood in his Austin office, his gnarled hands clasped behind his rheumatic back, as he stared at the map tacked to the kalsomined wall.

"Fentonville," he murmured. "First I've heard of her."

But McDowell did not need a map to help him visualize the great Lone Star State. As Chief of the Texas Rangers, and officially responsible for law and order in the State, he knew it from the Gulf coast to its farthest western reaches. In his long-gone youth, and before encroaching age had pinned him to a swivel chair, McDowell had ridden those danger trails himself, carrying Ranger justice, from the tamer eastern portions of Texas to the vast wild lands encompassing the Trans-Pecos and the Red River, the Colorado, the Nueces.

In his clever brain was the memory of every trail over which he had pursued outlaws and fugitives, while guns had roared and flamed over the red-earth plains of central Texas, the chaparral jungles of the Nueces, and the lush semi-tropical Gulf coast. He could picture the sandy flats, the red mud in the wet season, the choking dust in the dry, along the northern border where the wind blew all the way from the Arctic with nothing to stop it but some barbed wire fences in Kansas.

And he knew the strange Trans-Pecos, rising to ten thousand feet in the mountains, a tremendous semi-arid plateau split by dry canyons. He could vision the bottom lands choked with cactus and other thorny growths, and the great rocks thrusting to a hot, azure sky.

"I remember them Injun springs," he was musing now, as his rheumy eyes studied the map for which he had no need. " 'Cordin' to this letter I got from that feller named Fenton, that'll be where the town stands."

With a red pencil he made a small red cross at the spot across the Pecos where the new settlement must be.

McDowell's calm this day was an unusual thing. He had all the fieriness of disposition usually accredited to a Southern gentleman, like himself, and nothing frayed his temper so much as did reports of Texans being persecuted.

If a bandit held up some citizen who was returning home after an evening's diversion at some El Paso resort, McDowell heard of it. If a lonely cowboy, riding line to protect his employer's cattle, ran into rustler or raiding Indian guns, the report came to McDowell's desk. He needed no thermometer to gauge the temperature of Texas. He was so experienced that he could shuffle through a sheaf of police reports and tell to exactitude what point of fever his bailiwick had reached at the moment.

He touched the tinkle bell on his desk lightly, and a clerk came to the door, saluted, and stepped inside. The man looked anxiously at Captain Bill.

"Say, you sick today, Cap'n?" he asked.

"No, cuss yuh! Who said so? Why, I . . . Ahem!" McDowell caught himself just in time, and ordered in a quiet voice, "Please ask Ranger Jim Hatfield to come in."

Chin dropped, astounded at his Chief's soft voice and lack of temper, the clerk hurried away.

Soon a soft tread sounded in the corridor, and a tall man came into the room, his gray-green eyes worried as they sought McDowell's.

Ranger Jim Hatfield stood well over six feet in his polished, spurred half-boots. Because he was the man whom McDowell had mentally picked as his personal representative, Hatfield always was given the hard jobs.

As far as outward appearance went, Hatfield had none of the aspect of a quick-trigger fighting man — unless his keen eyes were studied closely. Instead, in his fresh blue shirt and red bandanna, with dark trousers tucked into boots that each had a lone star on its top, he seemed to be merely a good-natured cowboy.

The chinstrap of his big Stetson was loose in the runner about his square, rugged jaw. His hair was jet-black, with the sheen that told of health and youth. His legs were long and powerful, his shoulders broad, but the hips at which depended the cartridge belts supporting his twin, blue-steel Colts, were narrow. Bronzed by the Texas sun and winds, and strong as one of the State's granite cliffs, still Hatfield was no Greek god. But the hint of power innate in him was breath-taking.

Not that he was stern and severe, for his wide mouth somewhat relieved any severity his other features indicated. But in him appeared to be the rippling ferocity of a leashed panther, and McDowell knew that the man could move with devastating speed.

Hatfield's lazy slouch might have deceived others about his swiftness in a fight. But McDowell was aware that those slender hands of his top Ranger could reach, draw and fire the Colts from their supple, oiled holster with the speed of legerdemain.

"Mornin', Cap'n Bill." His voice, too, was lazy and drawling, low. Yet when necessary he could raise it until it could thunderously be heard against northers.

"Howdy, Hatfield, my boy," Captain Bill greeted. "Glad yuh're in. I got a letter here from an hombre named John Fenton. Appears he's head of a settlin' bunch of pioneers who've lit across the Pecos at the point marked on that map with a red cross — Fentonville they named it. New town. They done fine for a while, but rustlers have hit 'em. The owlhoots are led by Pecos Carns who likes to call hisself King of the Rustlers. I've had some other little reports on this Carns." Captain Bill grinned. "Jim," he said, "so long as that owlhoot seems determined to be king, it's up to the Rangers to crown him, I reckon."

Hatfield's gray-green eyes flicked to the

wall map, and the red mark McDowell had made, then back to his Chief.

"Cap'n," he said gently, and it seemed irrelevantly, "the boys say you ain't lost yore temper in two days! You sick?"

McDowell frowned, his frosty brows ferocious, his lips set. He cleared his throat and rattled John Fenton's letter.

"I ain't been better in twenty years," he declared, "though right now I feel like a dynamite bomb about to explode, Jim. Between you and me — I wouldn't want this to go no farther — I foolishly seen a sawbones recent, and he told me I'd live to be a hundred and twenty if I quit lettin' my temper get the better of me. That's all."

"I savvy." Hatfield looked relieved. He was mighty fond of McDowell, and any hint that the old man might not always be right where he was, hurt deeply.

"Listen to this," Captain Bill said, and read from the letter he held, " 'One of our ranchers, Hal Lewiston, was shot in cold blood by Carns' cattle thieves. Now my older son Nat is gone, killed by them, I'm shore, for he went to trail 'em. The rustlers are bold, rampant. One of my best friends, raided by the thieves and unable to pay his debts, has killed himself. We need help, and quick.' "

McDowell's voice shook. Suddenly he blew up, banging a fist on the desk so the bell and inkwell jumped. He swore with blasphemous fury.

"When I hear of folks bein' put on like that it makes me bile inside!" he bellowed. "Texans, my own people, bein' persercuted by a cussed band of mongrel cattle thieves who need hot lead in their innards! Ugh!"

Caught by his own frailties, McDowell collapsed in his chair, but grinned at Hatfield.

"Hah, now I feel better," he said. "Couldn't hold it no longer, Jim. If I went on like that, it'd seem like a hundred and twenty years in no time at all!"

McDowell, relieved by his natural outburst, gave Jim Hatfield detailed instructions, and just a little later, the old Chief watched from a window as Hatfield approached a magnificent golden sorrel. The mount danced a bit and nuzzled the Ranger's slim, caressing hand.

"That golden-hided cayuse and him are brothers," muttered McDowell.

Hatfield swung into saddle. Under one long leg a well-kept carbine was snugged in its boot. The saddle-bags contained iron rations and extra ammunition, and a poncho was rolled at the cantle. The tall

Ranger could live for weeks on the land, with a bit of salt, coffee and sugar from his pack in addition.

McDowell saw them off, westward for the Trans-Pecos. The old Ranger Captain felt almost as good as if he himself were riding Goldy on the way to carry Ranger justice to the wilderness. . . .

It was two weeks before Jim Hatfield reached the end of his journey, and the Trans-Pecos. It had been a swift, hard trip from Austin headquarters, but Hatfield and the sorrel knew how to make such runs, how to conserve strength for fighting at the end of a difficult march. North of the Edwards Plateau, they were nearing the deep canyon of the black-watered Pecos, headed for a crossing, when Hatfield straightened, peering toward the river.

"Now who's that ahead of us, Goldy?" he murmured.

Expert at trailing and always alert because of his calling, Hatfield had been somewhat slowed down during the past two hours. Faint dust in the air, the disturbed sandy rut of the trail, had told him that a man was riding ahead of him.

Natural caution required that he make sure of such a traveler's identity, especially when so near his goal. In a secret pocket was snugged the silver star on silver circle, emblem of the mighty Texas Rangers, but Hatfield did not make it a habit to flaunt his badge. For it was his custom, on beginning any investigation, to gain all pertinent facts before declaring himself an officer.

In that way he often gained valuable information and was well along toward solving his case before the enemy he was after was aware of his presence. When he met John Fenton he would reveal who he was, since Fenton had sent for Ranger assistance. But aside from that he expected to work under cover.

There were settlements to the north and south, at some distance off. Perhaps, Hatfield thought, the man who was riding ahead of him would turn off toward one of these.

Goldy moved up to a rise in the road, hoofs sliding on rocky footing. Stands of mesquite and pines clothed the hills. The sun was high in the blue sky, and gaudy-winged butterflies hovered over waxy flowers of a nearby bush. A road-runner emerged from the side of the trail and invited the rider to a game of chase-me.

The Ranger drew up at the top of the rise, and from this vantage point could see the country for about two miles westward.

It was thinly grassed, broken by woods and rocks. A few cows grazed on the north, and beyond them a thin plume of smoke indicated an isolated ranch. The east-west road ran on, to disappear in the next wavelike elevation, fringed with dark trees. There was a north-and-south path which no doubt led to the lonely ranch.

Now he could see the traveler who had delayed him. The fellow was riding a black mustang. He wore leather and a large Stetson, giving him the appearance of a rancher. He turned north onto the trail, at the crossroads. There was a crude sign there, made of a wooden slab fastened to a small tree trunk cut off for the purpose. A short way further on a thick clump of mesquite hid the west margin of the trail.

As Hatfield regarded this scene, abruptly a dark figure emerged from the mesquite, a man in black leather. The sun glinted on a Colt barrel. With a quick exclamation, the Ranger snatched at his own carbine, throwing a cartridge into the breech.

But the action ahead was too fast for it to be checked. For the rider chose to fight, ripping at his reins, seeking to draw his pistol. The man who had jumped him pulled trigger. The horseman sagged, fell out of saddle, and his weight stopped the startled horse so that the killer was able to seize the reins.

One of those swift, terrible tragedies of these lonely, dangerous spaces had been enacted, a desperate man killing another fellow being to obtain his horse and possessions.

Hatfield was already pushing Goldy on the down slope.

Busy searching the pockets of his victim, the fellow in the black leather was stooped over, and did not see the Ranger until Hatfield was within twenty-five yards of him. The vibration of the earth under the sorrel's hoofs warned him. With a quick oath he turned, his Colt, which he had laid down by him, flying to his hand.

"Throw down!" shouted the Ranger.

He had an impression of a sharp, long-nosed face, of vicious red-rimmed eyes. The man in black leather had not shaved for days, and every inch of him was savage. He was hardly human, but a predatory beast who destroyed decent folks.

Hatfield had to shoot, and quickly. That heavy Colt in the killer's hand was rising to pin him as he charged in. He held the carbine in his hands, guiding his mount with his knees, and Goldy steadied under him with the pressure. A spurt of dust kicked up a few feet ahead of the sorrel. The carbine crackled in the dry, warm air, and the man in black leather threw up both arms, turned once, and fell to the ground.

Chapter IV

Set-up

The killer was not playing possum. Hatfield's slug had neatly drilled the man's brain. There was a hole between the fading eyes, and another in the Stetson brim, which had been pushed back and down on the greasy head.

Hatfield dismounted, and coolly checked up.

He easily read the story. Off the trail, just hidden in the bush, lay a dead gray mustang, its flanks showing terrible spur gouges, its ribs showing the marks of the quirt. It had been pushed and beaten to death. The desperate killer, perhaps fleeing from a rope noose and the law, had managed to roll and drag the horse out of sight, and had awaited the coming of some victim who would supply him with a fresh mount.

The black mustang wore a ranch brand. Nearby lay the man who had ridden him, the man who, almost home, had been slain for his horse. He was a man of about forty, and about him were no marks of the owl-hoot brand. Among some papers Hatfield found on the ground, dropped there by the thief, the Ranger discovered the victim's probable identity — his name, his ranch brand, the Texas section in which he had lived.

The Ranger glanced speculatively north. The smoke from the ranchhouse was some miles away, and to take the body there would mean loss of half a day, and in an emergency which even now might be too far along for him to overcome. The living required his help.

He scratched a note of explanation on a sheet of paper, and pinned it to the dead rancher's shirt. Securing the body in the saddle, he started the black mustang off. The animal trotted up the trail, obviously knowing the way home.

Turning his attention to the bandit, Hatfield searched him. There was some money in his pockets, and other possessions of no import, but in the inner pocket of the black leather jacket was a soiled letter. Hatfield unfolded it and read:

Mete Acey Miles best man with long rope in Tex. C U nex month.

Mart

Checking the scrawled address on the outside again the Ranger made it out to be "Pecos Carns."

"Sounds like an interduction," he mused. "And this Carns is my meat."

He unfolded the letter and placed it in his shirt pocket for any future use he might find for it. "Acey" Miles had evidently been running from the Law, and had been on his way to join Carns' rustlers across the Pecos.

Fentonville and its terrible trouble called him, and he hurried on his way, hoping to cross the Pecos before night set in. . . .

In the yellow sunlight of the following forenoon, Jim Hatfield rode the golden sorrel into Fentonville. One glance sufficed to take in the little settlement, with its dozen structures, the store, the square wooden building with the sign that proclaimed it to be the headquarters of the "Central Pecos Development Co.," and that John Fenton was its president.

At the right was a smaller sign:

SILAS BARSTOWE — INVESTMENTS

The Pecos Inn attracted the Ranger — such an oasis was usually a good place to begin an investigation. It offered a thirsty rider refreshment even as he stood at the font of local gossip, the bartender.

Dropping reins over the hitch-rack, Hatfield approached the Pecos Inn. Before he could enter, a figure popped out to greet him.

"Howdy, stranger, howdy! Welcome to Fentonville. Mighty dry day, ain't it?"

The man seemed harmless, a Frontier mossyhorn with a wide, vacuous grin on his whiskery face. His clothing was tattered, and his felt hat had two holes in the crown.

It was Old Pete. A new arrival in town was usually good for at least one free drink, he always figured. He held open the door for the tall man, trailing him to the bar.

The saloon was empty at this hour save for a barkeeper. There were some crude tables and benches on the dirt floor, and the bar was a plank nailed to upright barrels, with a shelf on which stood bottles and glasses. A small keg was raised on sawhorses, and from it was dispensed the redeye whisky common to the Frontier.

"Set 'em up for two," ordered the Ranger, paying for Old Pete and himself.

Old Pete immediately became garrulous, his way of paying for the treat.

"Yes, suh, mighty nice town, mister — er — big feller," he said. "I didn't get yore handle but yuh're a gent, I can see it. I says to myself, 'Here comes a gent, a real gent, of the first water.'"

"And whisky," said the bartender, and winked.

"This is yore home town, I take it," Hatfield said to Old Pete.

"I've made it so. Last place I lived, I seen a feller standin' sort of shy-like on the saloon porch . . . Lessee, I believe it was a little town this side El Paso. I goes up to him and says, 'Mighty dry today, ain't it, mister?' He says, 'You think so, hey?' and pulls a hogleg and shoots right through my new hat. 'Twas new then."

Old Pete took off his felt, and ruefully stuck a finger through the two holes.

"That's the twelfth feller shot right through them same two holes, Pete," remarked the bartender.

"John Fenton about town this mornin'?" inquired Hatfield. "My handle is Miles — Ace Miles some call me. I was thinkin' of mebbe investin' in a section or two in these parts. Interested in ranchin'."

He thought it best to satisfy the barkeeper's curiosity at the start, to check speculation as to his identity.

"Fenton?" the barkeep said. "He's over at his office, I reckon. Seen him half an hour ago when he rode in from his home." The man behind the bar shook his head, soberly. "Poor John's failin' mighty fast. Since he lost his son he ain't been the same at all."

"I'll show yuh where Mr. Fenton is," said Old Pete eagerly.

"All right, Pete. S'pose we have another. It may be a dry walk."

Old Pete trotted ahead of the tall Ranger, unnecessarily acting as a guide to the office of the Central Pecos Development Company. Hatfield dismissed him at the door and, after knocking, stepped into the corridor.

To the left was an open entry, and a solidly built man of middle-age sat behind an oak desk. There were streaks of white through his brown hair, and his face was drawn, and thin. Dark lines were beneath his blue eyes which showed suffering as he looked at the tall officer. It touched Hatfield's heart.

"Yuh're John Fenton?" he asked.

He looked around, but there was no one else in the office, the walls of which were covered with maps of the immediate region, and various sections. There was a file in one corner, a chair or two, and a grass mat on the crude plank floor.

"I'm Fenton," the graying man said. "What can I do for yuh?"

Hatfield moved close to the desk. In his cupped hand lay the silver star on silver circle, emblem of the Texas Rangers.

"I'm Jim Hatfield, from Cap'n Mc-Dowell's headquarters at Austin," he said in a low voice. "We got yore call for help, Fenton."

Fenton stood up, to grip his hand. He was holding himself together by a great effort of will.

"I — I've hoped yuh'd come, Ranger. Mighty glad yuh're here. We're havin' a bad time of it. My own son's gone, as of course yuh know. It's a blow that's hard for a man to take."

"Nothin' worse. Yuh shore he's dead?"

"Fairly shore, but the uncertainty's killin' his mother and me. His hoss come home, the saddle gone. We know that Nat was trailin' this Pecos Carns gang, tryin' to find the killers of Hal Lewiston, one of our settlers. Figger they caught him on their sign and done him in."

Fenton gave Hatfield all the details at his command, concerning the thieves and killers who infested the range.

"You keep my arrival to yoreself, Fenton," warned the Ranger. "I like to work quiet-like till I'm shore of things. My handle is Ace Miles, if anybody asks — and I'm a cowman, lookin' for a Western range . . . In yore note to Cap'n Bill yuh said one of yore best friends had killed hisself."

"That was George Tate. He could never stand to owe anything, and the rustlers run off his cows so's he couldn't pay his debts. He drunk some strychnine. My boy Nat was sort of engaged to George's girl Emily. Fact is, I got Mrs. Tate and the kids with me now, at home. They're goin' to sell their ranch to settle up — Barstowe's promised to help. He's a mighty fine friend, is Si Barstowe. He give us all a hand startin' here."

"Barstowe? That'll be the investment man next door?"

John Fenton nodded. Stricken at the loss of his son, as well as by the other dark tragedies which had come upon the range, it was difficult for him to observe the usual amenities. His mind was still in a state of shock, and his big hands kept clenching, his nails digging into his palms.

"I'd like to meet Barstowe," Hatfield said. "Then I'll take a run out to yore ranch. I want to talk with the young lady, yore son's friend. She might be able to give me more of a line on what he was aimin' to do. And then, I can see somethin' of the country."

"I'll go out with yuh, then," Fenton told him. "There ain't much doin' in town just now. Come on. I'll introduce yuh to Barstowe, and tell him I'm leavin' the office here for the day."

Fenton was restless, glad to be able to move. He led Hatfield across the hall, through a connecting door into a well-furnished office occupying the south end of the square building. It was better furnished than the other, with a carpet, easy chairs, framed mottoes on the walls.

A man sat behind a flat-topped desk, a large man with thick, dark hair. His nose was broad, his teeth prominent, and side-burns adorned his pink cheeks. He wore a black frock coat.

Behind him stood a cabinet stocked with bottles of liquor and boxes of cigars. The smoke from a Cuban cheroot filled the air, mingling with the aroma of the brandy in the glass at his elbow.

"Barstowe," began Fenton, "this is — er —"

"Ace Miles, from the Red River, mister,"

broke in the Ranger loudly, thrusting a slim hand across the desk. He did not trust Fenton's memory. The rancher was too shaken to think straight.

Silas Barstowe's smile was benign, as he rose and shook hands. The gold-mounted bear tooth flapped gently on his well padded stomach as he welcomed the tall stranger to Fentonville.

"You're thinking of investing here, sir?" he asked, after offering the cigar box and brandy decanter to his guests.

Hatfield nodded, as he sat down. His manner was breezy, that of a successful cattleman. He knew how to play a part.

"Figgerin' on expandin' some, and buyin' in across the Pecos, Barstowe," he informed. "I heard tell of yore development here. Looks like good range, though I wonder how yore water'll hold up with a big herd."

"We can guarantee you so much flow," said Barstowe earnestly. "Up to this time we've dealt with small-scale cowmen. But I've thought that perhaps larger outfits might work better."

"Barstowe can help yuh with financial backin' if yuh'd need such," put in Fenton.

"Gladly," Barstowe nodded.

Hatfield was favorably enough impressed

by the banker and broker. From all Fenton had said, the man had helped the settlers, and was their friend. He saw nothing about the set-up to arouse his suspicions, and Barstowe had a benign, good-natured manner.

"Well, I'll be back in a day or two, Barstowe," Hatfield said, as he rose. "I'm ridin' out now with Fenton to look over some sections other side of his spread. See yuh later."

Pecos Carns called for the Ranger's attentions. The King of the Rustlers stood foremost in his mind as the man to locate first of all. He had the note "Acey" Miles had been carrying to Carns and hoped to use it.

Chapter V
Rustler Heaven

John Fenton saddled his mustang and he and Jim Hatfield left the settlement together. The sun was warm and a hot breeze rustled the dry brush as the Trans-Pecos rose in its savage grandeur before them.

"Carns has a hide-out northwest of here, but it's hard country to thread though," remarked Fenton.

As they rode along Hatfield drew out the story of the development, of the big springs which gave the settlers a good supply of water, and of Silas Barstowe's kindness in helping them get a start. All had apparently gone well until Pecos Carns had begun his depredations.

A few miles west of the town lay Fenton's ranch, with its oblong ranchhouse that was made of native timber and had a thatched roof. Hatfield's keen eyes saw the long wooden conduit that snaked from the nearby elevations, bringing water to Fenton's troughs and barnyard pool. Cattle grazed on the grass which covered the section.

All the buildings plainly were of recent construction, some of them not yet completed. There were some corrals, a barn and unfinished sheds, and gear stood about in the yard.

A young fellow with an eager face was at work with a mustang, but stopped to greet his father.

"My son, Jack Junior," introduced Fenton.

Jack shook hands with the guest, and took his father's horse to unsaddle the animal and rub the mustang down. Hatfield saw to his own mount, and when he strode to the open door of the house, Mrs. Fenton greeted him with a pleasant smile. Sue Fenton, the daughter of the house, a slim, dark beauty of sixteen, brought in a tray of cookies and cool drinks.

The house was crowded to capacity. John Fenton ceremoniously introduced Hatfield as "Ace" Miles to each occupant in turn. Hatfield shook hands with George Tate's widow, with young Sam Tate, and with the fragile-looking yellow-haired Emily. The girl's young eyes were sad, and the Ranger was touched with pity for these people who mourned the loss of George

Tate and Nat Fenton.

Em, he quickly learned, had been the last person to see Nat before he had ridden away, headed toward Pecos Carns' hideout. Hatfield drew her aside, to question her about young Fenton's moves. She was sure that Nat had trailed the rustlers, and no doubt run upon them, to be shot down in the ensuing battle.

The Ranger was weary from the long run to Fentonville, and Goldy needed rest and feed. He spent the night at Fenton's ranch. Early the next morning, with a warm breakfast under his belt and a rough estimate of the surrounding country in his mind, he rode toward the wilds in which Pecos Carns supposedly lurked.

"They may keep a look-out on guard, and we got to be careful how we approach," he told Goldy.

Animal tracks, of horses shod and unshod, of stray cattle, crisscrossed the many trails and winding paths. The country a few miles northwest of Fenton's rose steeply, and the canyon of the Pecos curved that way.

Deep side ravines, choked with brush and rocks, blocked the direct route along the main stream, so it was necessary to detour far inland to cross these. At the bottoms ran little feeders, carrying off the topsoil. When the rains came in the mountains, these channels were often raging torrents.

When the Ranger decided that he was in the vicinity of Carns' mysterious hide-out — it might lie anywhere in that dense swale of thorned brush and tortuous ravines — he sought a high point from which to observe the surrounding terrain. Leaving the sorrel below, he climbed the last two hundred feet to the peak and searched the wild scene with his field-glasses.

The sun was high, yellow and warm, and birds and insects were around in abundance. He could see traces of smoke in the intensely blue sky, back toward Fentonville, marking the various ranches, but there wasn't the slightest sign of smoke or anything else that might help him in his hunt for the rustler stronghold. He needed to know more about its location before he could move.

"Nothin' to do but wait," he murmured.

The afternoon passed fruitlessly. Nothing human disturbed the wilderness quiet. Night came on, and finally the Ranger slept, rolled in his blanket, his head on his saddle.

Next morning, he was again sweeping the country with his glasses. It was around ten o'clock when he saw a line of riders coming along a deer trail from the dense woods to the northwest. There were eight of them, leather-clad men who were well-armed.

They passed about a half a mile from his eyrie, evidently heading for the cattle range near the Pecos.

When they had passed out of his sight, Hatfield went down, saddled Goldy, and started to backtrack on the band's trail. Now he had something fresh to work on. In a soft spot he found a hoofmark with a cross made of nails — "to keep the devil away" as the saying went.

The way was narrow, and thorny branches reached out to scratch the rider and the golden sorrel.

He missed the turnoff, but soon realized the trail was cold, and retraced his course. A broken twig in the dense face of a thicket drew him, and he found the opening to the blind path. It was cut to within fifty yards of the exit, a packed trail which slanted down into a creek ravine. There was a rocky run some yards above the level of the low-watered brook, as the canyon walls deepened when they neared the juncture with the Pecos.

It was ultra-dangerous, following that trail. Hatfield knew that such men as used it might shoot a strange traveler before challenging him.

A huge shoulder of gray-brown rock loomed ahead of him. He slowed the golden sorrel but had to pass the narrows, as the ravine, overgrown above, turned in its course.

"Reach!"

The challenge came as the Ranger pushed Goldy around the turn.

He put up his hands, and Goldy halted. On a rock ledge just over the trail crouched a man with a carbine in his hands, aimed at Hatfield's heart.

"I'm a friend," said the Ranger coolly. "Lookin' for Pecos Carns."

"Yeah? What's yore handle — and how do yuh savvy Carns is here?"

"I go by the name of Miles — and I come a long way to see Pecos, feller. A pard of his told me where I'd find him. How long yuh goin' to keep up this foolishness? My arms are gettin' tired."

His surety of tone, the explanation, did the trick. The carbine still pinned him but the challenger's voice was less gruff as he asked:

"Got any identerfication?"

"A letter to Carns from Mart. Want to see it?"

"Get it out . . . Careful now, how yuh reach for it."

Hatfield drew out the note. He placed it on the rock shelf, and the other man picked it up and read it.

"All right," he growled. "Yuh can ride ahead of me. I'll take yuh in."

The Ranger moved slowly on. Around the bend, the stream cut close under a sheer rock wall, but the south bank was a series of shelflike steps where some grass and small trees had been able to gain roothold. In this park, made by Nature, animals could be quartered, and nestling above high-water mark at the widest part of the top shelf, with one of its walls formed by the crumbling rock cliff, was the roomy home of Pecos Carns and his men.

It was an ideal spot, thought the Ranger, as he quickly sized up the surroundings. They had fresh water from the creek, protection from the elements, and it would take an army to rush that narrow gap.

No doubt they could retreat to the Pecos in a pinch. The cliffs hid them, and far above were dense thorn woods screening the steep, descending rock shelves. Smoke from the stone chimneys would be broken and dissipated by the overhanging lip, or carried through the ravine by the natural draft.

The main building had stone foundations, built high, and cemented with mortarlike mud. The upper parts of the walls were logs, the roof of thatched branches. In the front was a stone terrace where some supplies in boxes and bales lay about, evidently not yet stored away in the sheds farther away. The square windows had no glass, but there were crude shutters which could be closed against the cold and storms.

Hatfield did not see any cattle around, save for half a dozen dead cows hung from scaffolds, slaughtered beeves to be used as food.

"Reckon they don't fetch stolen herds here," he mused. "Prob'ly run 'em straight to their Mexican market."

"Hey, Carns — yuh got company!" sang out the sentry who had brought Hatfield in.

The stentorian shout echoed back and forth from the high walls, and woke up the place. Some men down by the corrals turned to stare. Others appeared at windows in the house, and several came out on the terrace. Among them was Pecos Carns. Hatfield was sure of that from the description he had been given of Pecos.

The raw-boned rustler chief, his bricky hair awry, was yawning as he emerged. He had obviously been napping. His carroty hair was unmistakable now, for he wore no hat. But he was wearing a Colt in the holster of his single cartridge belt which apparently he had not removed while he slept, and his black pants and blue shirt were rumpled.

Carns was not a prepossessing man. His nose was turned up, his mustache and hair of the same blazing hue, and his big hands and protruding joints, which Hatfield noticed as he dismounted and moved toward the house, made the chief gangling and awkward.

Carns' emerald eyes met the tall Ranger's. The rest of the men all regarded him very stolidly.

"He's got a note from Marty Bell, Boss," said the guard with Hatfield.

Pecos Carns bobbed his head. He accepted the letter and read it with a little difficulty, his lips spelling out the words. When he spoke, his voice was harsh, even though he probably meant to be polite.

"So yuh're Acey Miles. Glad yuh come, pard. Come on inside and we'll palaver. Shaky, you go on back to yore post."

Hatfield was relieved. He had passed the first dangerous inspection. He had not shaved, in order to have the proper shaggy appearance, and he knew how to act the part of a vicious outlaw, for he had come up against many such gentry in his work as a Texas Ranger. His role was not suspected, so far.

He followed Pecos Carns inside. Carns' rustlers watched him. Some were, perhaps, naturally jealous of the new arrival, vying as they did for their chief's favor. The size of this Acey Miles, his sureness, the way he wore his guns and his general appearance, were a challenge to some of the quarrelsome natures in the outlaw camp. But that was to be expected.

Chapter VI
Human Dog

Pecos Carns took Hatfield into the square central room, which occupied about half of the building. It was fairly well furnished. There were some rough chairs, a table, an oak cupboard containing bottles and glasses, and a bright-colored Mexican grass mat was on the rough board floor. Bunks stood along the walls. There were a couple of oil lamps, some candles in holders, and other odds and ends which either had been purloined or purchased somewhere by the bandits. Doors opened from the big room into others, and at the rear was a kitchen where a wood-burning stove was visible. One of the side doors was shut.

Pecos Carns went to the cupboard and brought out a bottle of whisky and two tin cups. He poured drinks, and downed his own at a single gulp, smacking his lips over it.

"Good rotgot, Miles," he said. "Help yoreself."

Carns sat down opposite the tall Ranger, and again ran his green eyes quickly up and down the powerful figure of the recruit.

"I like yore looks, son," he said. "Yuh got the set of a real fightin' man. Lot of these mavericks that call themselves hard are yeller coyotes that quit in a pinch. Me, I pick and choose my boys. I told Marty never to send me anybody who ain't first class."

Hatfield nodded. He drank the burning liquid which Carns had poured for him, and smacked his lips.

"Marty told me how to get here — Boss. I was workin' over there, but my face got too familiar. Thought I better cool off a while in other parts. Yuh savvy how it is."

Pecos Carns nodded soberly. "That's the trouble back East. Too many sheriffs and too many people yellin' their fool heads off. No place for a man to rest up. Here, it's different. We got a nice set-up. Right now, we're workin' on a big proposition."

"Cattle?"

"Well, sort of, though the cows ain't the main angle. We'll go into it later. Have another."

"Don't care if I do."

"When I seen Marty last month he

promised to send me some good men," continued Carns. "So far we've managed to keep our hide-out secret. Have any trouble findin' the way through?"

"I'd never have made it," assured Hatfield, "if I hadn't savvied where to look. I rode by half a dozen times before I picked up the blind trail."

"Yeah," Carns nodded, pleased. "Even when yuh line up that bald peak and the twin ones it's tough to locate it."

There were others in the house somewhere. Hatfield was aware that sharp eyes were regarding him, perhaps through peepholes. And he could hear vague stirrings in rooms at the sides.

Then the closed door was unlatched, and someone emerged. Hatfield glanced around. He was surprised to see a girl in a red silk gown walking across the floor.

Her black hair was dressed high on her arrogantly lifted head, and held with a jeweled Spanish comb. She may have had some Spanish blood, but in general appearance she was Anglo-Saxon. She was a big girl with large brown eyes and a clear complexion which had been touched up with rouge. She moved slowly, with a deliberate attempt to accentuate her ample curves. Pretty and attractive as she was, her gaze was bold as she met Hatfield's with an appraising flirtatious smile.

Pecos Carns gave a short nod of his red-haired head.

"Hullo, sweetheart," he said to the girl, and to Hatfield, "Miles, this is my woman, Filly. Her handle's Philomena but that's too long to bother with. Set down, honey, and have a drink. Yore purty tonsils must be dry."

"Glad to know you, mister," she purred. "What'd you say the lad's name is, Peeky?"

"Miles, Acey Miles."

Hatfield got up, swept off his Stetson, and bowed low. The girl seemed to like this show of gallantry for she smiled, her even white teeth gleaming between her full red lips. She sat down on Carns' knee, and patted his rough cheek.

"Is my bitsy naughty boy aw right today? He dwank an awful lot of whisky last night!"

Philomena's voice was as bold as her eyes. She hadn't the slightest self-consciousness or maidenly modesty in her make-up. The spectacle of the girl talking baby talk to the fierce killer nearly threw Hatfield off his guard. It was so ludicrous that he just managed to stifle his laughter and maintain a sober face.

"Oh, I can drink a barrel and never feel it," boasted Carns. "How about you, Filly? You drunk ev'rybody else under the table."

"My head aches — poor Filly!" She snuggled up close to Carns and he kissed her on the temple. "That's right — make it better, Peeky."

"We'll have another party tonight," said Carns, "to celebrate Miles' jinin' up. Carve some fresh steaks."

"I'd like to take care of my hoss, Carns," said Hatfield, when they had finished the second round of drinks. "He's had a long, hard run of it over here."

"Bueno. I'll call one of the boys and have him show you the ropes . . . Hey, Brownie!"

A stout rustler with a round head and stringy brown hair answered the summons.

"This is Acey Miles, Brownie," Carns said. "He's goin' to be with us for a while. He's a first-class man with a rope. Show him around."

Hatfield bowed again to the good-looking Filly, who winked at him behind Carns' back as he left with "Brownie."

The stout man took him outside. Some distance from the main house were some huts. A couple had padlocks on the doors. No doubt they contained ammunition and

68

liquor. There was a saddle shed, and other adjuncts necessary to the rustler trade and living in the wilds.

"So yuh're jinin' up with us, Miles?" said Brownie, tentatively.

"Yeah. Looks like a nice spread yuh got here. Good fellers and all."

Brownie nodded. "It's all right. Carns is a bangup chief. Only one thing to be careful of."

"What's that?"

"Don't show that Filly gal any attention. Just say 'Howdy, ma'am,' and let it go at that. She's got a wanderin' eye, specially when she's likkered up, but Carns is jealous and quick to fight over her. There's other women around that are a lot safer."

Hatfield thanked Brownie for the advice. The stout man showed him around the big camp, introducing him to several rustlers who were at work here and there. He helped the Ranger unsaddle and rub down the golden sorrel, and they turned Goldy loose in the natural park near at hand.

In the distance, a faint but steady sound persisted in the eardrums.

"That's the Pecos, ain't it?" asked Hatfield, after a while.

"That's it," said Brownie. "On'y a quarter mile down the canyon. Little rapids makes the hum you hear."

Hatfield noted a narrow path twisting on along the bottom of the creek canyon toward the mother stream, but did not appear to give it any special attention. When he and Brownie had taken care of Goldy and made the rounds of the rustler stronghold, they went back toward the main house, Hatfield with his blanket and saddle on his shoulders.

"House is full up," said Brownie. "Yuh can sleep in one of the sheds or outdoors if yuh've a mind to."

The Ranger went around to the rear of the house, with Brownie trotting at his heels. The cliff formed the back wall, but there was a space between the uneven rock and the foundation, and Hatfield stopped short as he saw legs and bare feet that were scarred by cuts, sticking from under the place. He saw that a length of rusty bear-chain which was fastened to an iron staple driven into a crack in the stone disappeared under the house, and he believed it was attached to the still figure of the man whose legs he saw.

Brownie didn't say anything. He seemed to take the legs for granted. He showed Hatfield where to stow his gear, and a dry spot beneath an overhanging ledge where he might sleep.

"Reckon I'll snatch a few winks now, Brownie," the masquerading Ranger said. "I had a long run over."

"All right. Yuh want anything, let me know. We'll have chow before dark sets in. Just come over and pitch in."

Hatfield was glad of a chance to rest, to think things over. The sun slanted off, and shadows fell over the creek canyon. There was the steady, lulling sound of the running river, the voices of men now and then, the chirp of birds. He heard a horse whinny from the park. Then he dozed off. When he woke later, it was to find that men had come in and were parking their saddles in the shed. A couple of cooks were busy and the odor of broiling beefsteak mingled with the delicious aroma of coffee reached his nostrils, making him realize his hunger.

Men with tin mugs and plates were gathering around the cookshed, waiting for the hand-out. Hatfield saw Brownie and joined the group. Other rustlers eyed him, then Brownie introduced him to "Jack," and to "Billy" and "Kansas Joe," "Mex" and the rest. They were in leather or other clothing meant for hard wear, and some wore their Stetsons. All had on guns and in their bronzed faces was something which showed them to be quick shots and hard riders.

When his turn came, Hatfield received a thick cut of beef, a mug of steaming coffee, some chunks of homemade bread. Using his knife as his only implement he made a satisfactory meal, sitting on a flat rock beside Brownie.

Dark was at hand. Oil lamps and lanterns were lighted, and Pecos Carns' home stood out against the blackness of the high protecting cliffs against which it was built.

The party began an hour later. There were about thirty of Carns' men at the hide-out at the moment. Hatfield understood that other crews were out, working. Besides Filly, the red-haired chief's sweetheart, there were four other girls, one of them an Indian, another a Mexican. Filly was the best looking of them all.

Brownie had an accordion, and another rustler played the fiddle. There was plenty of whisky, and immediately they began to tank up. Some of the men danced with the girls, though all studiously avoided Filly, who sat with Pecos Carns. Carns, impressed by Hatfield's size and appearance, and the borrowed reputation he had as Acey Miles, also kept the tall recruit near him, pressing drinks upon him.

As the liquor took hold, the party grew more boisterous. Heavy-booted feet shook the whole building as they danced about to the music of the accordion and the squeaky fiddle. Filly was right in her element. She boldly whirled about the room in Carns' arms, laughing, flirtatious.

"Let's have some sport, boys, with the dog!" shouted Pecos Carns after a time. "Mex, go unchain him."

A vaquero went out the side way, and Pecos Carns began to whistle as one might call a hound. Hatfield, expecting to see an animal bound through the door, watched as Carns took down a quirt, and a man or what had been a man, came into the room, blinking in the bright light.

He was bent, and shuffled rather than walked. His clothing was torn, stained, hardly recognizable as such, just dirty rags. His hair was matted and touseled, his eyes sunk deep, but were staring, filled with terror. It was an animal-like terror. Scabs and dirt covered his face.

"Down, Rover, yuh bad dog!" cried Carns, making a pass at him with the whip.

The creature cowered and went down on all fours. The Ranger was disgusted, filled with fury, but the outlaws laughed as the pitiful, obviously feeble-minded thing trembled and stared at the brutal rustler.

Kansas Joe jumped in and kicked him with a hard boot toe.

"Bark, cuss yuh! Growl at him, Rover."

Afraid of Carns and the quirt, the man gave several caninelike growls and barks. He feigned to snap at hands thrust at his face. They bedeviled him, teasing him as they would a harried dog.

They were all drunk by this time, including Carns and Filly. The rustler leader put out his boot.

"Lick it!" he ordered, and the man on all fours obeyed.

After a few minutes of further abasement, Carns tired of the sport. He slashed the human dog with his quirt, and Brownie chased him out, rechaining him.

It was the sort of cruel sport which would appeal to such men. Sadistic, egotistical, they enjoyed torturing others.

The grin was frozen on the Ranger's features. He had seen enough to judge what he had to face in trying to aid Fenton and the other ranchers. Carns and his men were capable of killing any number of the settlers.

Yet Pecos Carns had hinted at a "big proposition," something beyond ordinary rustling and gunning of victims on the range. Hatfield felt safe enough, for the time being, since he had passed the initial test, and he hoped to learn more of Carns' plans by remaining in the hide-out for a day or two more.

Chapter VII

Black Night

Around midnight, with the rustlers whooping it up, howling and stamping, and while Brownie was playing the accordion, there was a stir at the front door. A man whom Hatfield hadn't seen before came in, and approached Pecos Carns. Carns was sitting with Filly on his knee, singing a drunken refrain.

The new arrival was one of the bunch, but he was sober. He came to Carns and handed him an envelope.

Pecos Carns blinked, shaking his head. He spilled Filly off his knee as he shifted, to take the letter out and read it. He was none too fast a reader, and his lips worked as he spelled out each word.

Hatfield, curious as to what the message might contain, and on his guard in the enemy stronghold, edged closer to Carns. The rustler read aloud, each word an effort for him.

"A — Tex-as — Rang-er is head-ed —

yore — way" Carns paused, cleared his throat, and had a drink from his bottle before continuing. "He is six-foot-three — black hair — gray-green eyes — posin' — as — cattleman — name of Miles —"

Pecos Carns suddenly broke off. He turned his neck stiffly, and his emerald eyes fixed on Hatfield, who stood within two yards of him.

"Why, that's you!" he screeched.

Only the fact that the outlaws were drunk saved Hatfield's life. Pecos Carns had removed his gun-belt and laid it on the table. He threw himself forward, to snatch a Colt from the holster and kill the spy, the intruder who had dared penetrate to the heart of his camp. Two or three others, near Carns, had heard the letter, and realized what was going on. But they, too, were slower than usual because of the liquor they had imbibed.

Filly, sitting on the floor, began to scream shrilly, with fright.

"Don't shoot — you'll hit me!"

The Ranger was moving swiftly for the side door. The front was blocked by a mass of his enemies, and the sober outlaw who had brought the warning was making a draw. The other women began to shriek in concert and sympathy with Filly. Stunned,

Brownie and the rest, who did not yet know what was happening, watched with dropped jaws as the swift action flared.

Hatfield had several jumps to go before he could leap out the eastern exit of the house. He had to shoot for Carns, teeth clenched viciously and his face flaming, was determined to kill him.

Men stood now between the rustler chief and the Ranger. Carns had pulled himself together, shocked by the news of the spy in their midst. He did not miss the flash of the slim Ranger hand, and he threw himself off his chair with a squeak, shooting quickly. But his aim was bad, shaken by his own instinctive move to save himself.

The Ranger felt the cut of a bullet which just kissed his left arm. His return missed Carns by a foot as the rustler rolled under the table.

The room was a bedlam of women's shrieks, of aroused, cursing men.

"Get him!" bellowed Pecos Carns. "Down him!"

Hatfield fired into the lamps. Two shots cracked them, and he smashed a lantern hanging from an iron peg in the wall, near the door with his sweeping Colt barrel. Only breaths had elapsed since he had started his escape.

He threw himself backward out of the door, fell to the ground, rolling over and over. Bullets began whirling through the open door, but he was out of direct range. Scrambling to his feet, he began to run full-tilt along the path down the creek. To have tried to pass the front of the house would have been suicide, for already men were spewing from the door, looking for him. And the narrow pass was always guarded.

The Ranger could feel the warm blood flowing from the flesh wound in his left arm. He reloaded his revolver, glanced back at the buildings. It was as dark as pitch. He could see only a few stars, high up and directly over the gorge.

Shrill whistles came from his lips as he called Goldy, his trained sorrel. There was no time to hunt his gear but perhaps he would be able to work his horse out.

There had been some shock from the wound but he fought against the weakness, his powerful body carrying him on. Goldy would come to him, follow him. He whistled once more, so that the sorrel would be able to place him, scent him and come after him.

The ravine deepened, with the walls almost sheer as he neared the Pecos. He slipped off the path now and again, stumbling on the sharp rocks, cutting the hand which he kept out to guide and balance himself. Once he went into the shallow water of the creek.

He heard heavy splashings behind him, and stopped, to look back. Spots of light showed where rustlers with lanterns were slowly moving, hunting him in the darkness. They had figured he would try to rush the gate and this had given him a head start. It was Goldy making those splashings, and the ghostly shape of his sorrel overtook him. The horse was in the creek, making his way through the sand and rocky bed.

"Come on boy, we got to try it," muttered the Ranger as he moved on. "Only way."

The sound of the rapids in the main stream grew louder. Now he made a final turn, and beyond the bend saw the larger river, the black-watered Pecos. A slice of moon gilded the riffles of the rapids, but the Pecos was low in the summer heat. He reached its bank, standing on beaten sand.

Over the river, the rock walls rose high, forbidding. He could not get out there. And there was a drop here, where the creek came in. The Pecos spilled for a couple of hundred yards down a series of rocky steps, its own canyon walls steep, hemming it in. Hatfield slipped, went down, wet to the shoulder as he put out his injured left arm to break his fall.

With difficulty, the Ranger began wading downstream. Goldy, too, had trouble negotiating the slippery bottom, but the sorrel slowly trailed Hatfield.

For an hour, resting now and again when he found a dry spot along the river bank, the Ranger waded down the Pecos, sometimes with the water to his armpits. He kept hunting a way out, hunting some break in the walls.

He was sure there must be an escape route known to Carns and his men. But it was black dark, and he thought he might have missed the exit in the murk. It might be a hairpin path winding up and along the opposite bank. Or it might, conceivably, have been above the point where he had emerged when he had run from the bandit guns.

At last he came to a narrows where there was no ledge along which to crawl. He tried wading but the pushing dark water grew deeper. He held his gun-belts over his head, to keep them dry, as the river ringed his neck.

"Got to swim for it," he muttered. "Come on, Goldy."

The sorrel was willing. He launched himself into deep water and swam downstream, with Hatfield clinging with one hand to the mane of the powerful gelding. Then there came a turn in the gorge and the walls broke away. The Ranger could see the star-studded sky, and a strip of moon.

"The ford!" he mumbled.

It was the spot where he had crossed the Pecos on his way to Fentonville. It was north of the settlement, and there was a trail up which horses could be taken.

Once out of the canyon, Hatfield mounted bareback. Knowing his way now, he headed for Fenton's home.

The sky was paling behind him when he reached the yard and slid off. He was exhausted, blood had clotted on his arm wound, and the limb was stiff. He needed sleep and hot food.

John Fenton opened the back door of the house, and came out in pants and shirt and bare feet. There were deep lines under his tortured eyes.

"Ranger Hatfield!" he exclaimed. "What happened to yuh?"

Hatfield's clothing was torn and dripping. His bare left arm was held crooked, and stiff, but he was trying to rub down Goldy, thinking first of his horse.

"I been to call on Pecos Carns," he told the rancher.

"Yuh mean yuh located the rustler hide-out?"

"That's right. I was doin' fine, till a message come in describin' me. Then all tarnation busted loose."

"Lemme give yuh a hand with yore hoss," Fenton said, and helped him attend to Goldy.

After a rub-down, they turned the sorrel loose, and Fenton led the way into the kitchen. There was a fire going in the iron cookstove, and a pot of hot coffee was on it. On the board table in the center of the room a lantern burned low. Plainly Fenton had not been to bed, even though the new day was at hand, and gray light was spreading over the range. For a tin mug half-filled with coffee was on the table, and near the mug a picture in a silver frame.

"I've had trouble sleepin' since the boy was lost," explained the rancher simply. "That's Nat's pitcher there . . . Wait, I'm goin' to fetch some dry duds for you."

He left the kitchen, and soon returned with a pair of brown pants and a khaki shirt, as well as a pair of big boots. Hatfield was sitting at the table, drinking a cup of hot coffee, and staring at the picture of Nat Fenton. A boyish face looked from the faded photograph, a smooth-cheeked young fellow with fine eyes and a wide grin.

"He was seventeen when that was took," explained the father.

"Where'd he get that scar on his temple?" asked Hatfield.

"He was always an adventurous cuss," Fenton said fondly. "He was only a shaver when he tried to mount a crazy outlaw bronc, and that's what he got. His mother and me was mighty worried for a few days, but he got over it. Hoof cut him there."

Hatfield consumed the cold meat and bread which Fenton set before him. The food tasted delicious and restored him. No one else in the house was awakened as Fenton, worried about the Ranger's wound, washed the arm with warm water and soap and then bound it with a soft cloth. Feeling more relaxed, Hatfield rolled himself a quirly from Fenton's "makin's" and lighted up.

The Ranger deeply pitied John Fenton. The loss of his elder son had shaken the rancher terribly, and he was unable to throw off the shock of it. His suffering was acute.

"Where did you find Pecos Carns?" inquired Fenton, when Hatfield had been made comfortable.

"Down in a crik canyon not far back from the Pecos. They got blind trails in, and a guard on it. But now I savvy where it lies. Fenton, who'd yuh tell that I was here?"

"What?" Fenton looked troubled, startled.

"Someone spilt the beans that a Ranger had come to these parts, and give Carns an exact description of me. It near finished me off. Yuh're the only man I told my real identity to. Yuh must have told somebody — yore wife, yore best friend?"

Fenton passed a hand across his brow.

"No . . . Now, wait! Come to think of it, I did tell Silas Barstowe yesterday. But I trust him above myself. Barstowe asked where yuh'd gone to. Yuh'll remember yuh told him yuh was interested in investin' here. I had to explain to him."

"Huh. You put a lot of stock in this Barstowe, don't yuh?"

"He's our benefactor, Hatfield. He helped us get a start. Lent us money, assisted us in every way. Why, I look on him like he was an older brother. Yuh can't believe he was the one who sent that warnin' to Pecos Carns, a dirty outlaw!"

The Ranger shrugged. But Fenton was so certain of the broker's integrity that Hatfield, as yet only beginning his work in the district, and having met Barstowe but once and only for a few minutes, was almost convinced.

"Mebbe somebody's spyin' on yuh, Fenton," he said, "and heard yuh tell Barstowe I'm a Ranger. Or Barstowe might have told another person and it leaked out. Anyways, I'll check up after I've had some shut-eye. You goin' to yore office today?"

"I reckon. I'll ride in later."

"Say nothin' 'bout me bein' here, not even to Barstowe, savvy? I want yore word of honor."

"Yuh have it."

There was a warm, soft spot in the hay in Fenton's barn, and Hatfield chose it as a sleeping place. Fenton pointed out a saddle and gear that he might borrow, since he had lost his equipment at Carns' stronghold, and went on back to the house.

Chapter VIII

"Many a Slip"

It hadn't taken Hatfield long to fall asleep. Now, as he awoke he discovered that the sun, beating down on the stable roof, was heating the place like an oven. He felt rested though. His arm was still stiff but the wound had closed well.

Fenton had gone to town, but the women knew he was there, and Jack, Fenton's younger son, was watching for him when he emerged from the barn.

"Howdy, mister," sang out Jack. "Ma says to come right in when yuh're ready. She's got a meal waitin'. Pop says yuh're to have anything yuh want in the way of gear, so just say the word."

"Thanks, Jack."

With the Fenton youth was Sam Tate, Emily's brother. The death of his father had sobered Sam, who felt that he was now the head of the family. His boyish eyes, however, sparkled with admiration as he regarded the mighty figure of Hatfield.

"If I can help yuh, mister, let me know," he said.

"Much obliged, Sam," said the Ranger, then turned to young Fenton. "Yore dad said I could borrer a hull and bridle, Jack. I do need a carbine and some ammunition for such, if there's one kickin' around."

"Yuh can have mine!" cried Sam Tate, turning to run to the house and fetch the weapon. "It's a new 'un — was Pop's."

They were all hospitable folks. Em Tate, pretty as a painting, but with saddened eyes because of the terrible bereavements she had suffered, greeted the Ranger when he entered the homey kitchen, and Mrs. Fenton had a smile for him.

"Sit down, and start eating," she ordered. "You must be starved."

"I could eat a couple of hosses, I reckon," drawled the Ranger.

They had a pitcher of cider cooled by water, and home-made pats of butter to spread on the fresh bread they had baked that morning. Slices of meat, pork-and-beans, and other delicacies went well with the Ranger, who more than did justice to the food.

Fenton's home was a pleasant spot. The sun came in the wide, low windows, and the touch of the women, who were such wonderful home-makers, was everywhere apparent. There were some wildflowers arranged in a vase on the table, and white curtains tied back with ribbons. Dishes and pans shone, and the floor had just been scrubbed.

The big Ranger sat with his long legs stretched under the kitchen table, said "Yes'm" and "No'm," as Mrs. Fenton talked to him about this and that. "No'm," he had no family. "Yes'm," everything was fine. "No'm," it wasn't true that the food wasn't much account, just something she had had to serve because there was nothing else in the house.

Em Tate didn't have so much to say. She waited on him, but the sadness in her eyes showed she was mourning Nat and her father.

Now and then, when Jim Hatfield enjoyed such an interlude in a Texan's home during his dangerous expeditions, he felt that he was missing a great deal by being a rolling stone, without a home and a wife. But the work which he did was far too perilous to ask a girl to share such an existence. At any moment he might die under outlaw guns. And he was constantly on the move from one spot to another. He had to travel alone.

When he had been stuffed to repletion, eating more than he wanted, to please Mrs. Fenton, he thanked the women and took his leave of them. Jack and Sam were waiting for him in the yard. They had a fine carbine for him and a belt filled with ammunition for it, and the saddle and gear were ready.

They admired the powerful golden gelding tremendously, as they watched the Ranger saddle up. He said good-by to them then and left, but he turned to wave to them as he hit the trail for Fentonville.

"Nice folks, Goldy," he murmured. "Shame they have to be put upon by such scum as Pecos Carns."

The range had a quiet, peaceful aspect. Butterflies and birds winged in the warm sunshine of the afternoon and the Ranger could see pools of water and irrigation ditches, fed from the dam in the hills, and cattle grazing on the tough but nutritious grasses.

People could be happy here, if allowed to. But Nat was gone and that had broken Fenton and his wife, and hurt Em Tate to the core of her heart. George Tate was dead, too, and this had stricken another family of the type that were the backbone of the State.

There were other such families here also — hard-working parents toiling from morning till night, but joyfully to bring up their children. The settlers of this section were not wealthy or even well-off. From what John Fenton had told Hatfield they had come with their small savings but a large capacity for hard work to build their fortunes. It was such people that Mc-Dowell and his Rangers had to protect from predatory beasts.

Peaceful as the range looked, however, Hatfield kept a sharp watch. For he knew that appearances could be deceptive. The rustlers might possibly believe he had drowned in the river during the attempted escape from their stronghold, but they would be looking for either his body or him. A dry-gulcher's bullet from the next bush might punctuate a promising young Ranger's career.

Fenton's lay to the west of the settlement, and the shadow of the rider bobbed ahead, elongated and irregular because of Goldy's movements. The run to town was uneventful though, and soon the little settlement was before him. He rode in, waved to Old Pete, who stood slumped against the saloon.

Fenton's office door was open, and there

were two horses outside it, one belonging to Fenton. At the other wing of the square building was Silas Barstowe's office, and Hatfield, interested in the broker, dropped his reins in the shade at that side. In a three-sided shed to the rear stood a shining black buggy and a tethered horse, Barstowe's rig.

A side window was open, and Hatfield looked through it. Barstowe was sitting at his desk, smoking. He saw the tall figure pass the window, and gave a quick wave. Hatfield opened the door, as he heard Barstowe sing out, "Come in, sir," after his knock.

Barstowe rose, beaming upon him, thrusting out his well-fleshed hand.

"Delighted to see you, young man. Sit down, sit down. Have a cigar."

He pushed the box toward the Ranger.

"Obliged, Barstowe."

Hatfield sat down, opposite the broker with the benevolent face and expansive smile.

"Lovely country in these parts, isn't it?" Barstowe said. "Too bad we've had so much trouble. These rustlers are like a pack of wolves, sir."

"Fenton told yuh why I'm here, Barstowe," said the Ranger.

His gray-green eyes were fixed on the

other man, as he tried to size him up. The warning sent Pecos Carns had disturbed Hatfield's confidence in Barstowe, although Fenton was certain of the banker.

"Mebbe Fenton's right," the Ranger thought. "He might've been overheard. It's likely enough that Carns'd have a spy in the town."

Barstowe was either innocent or an excellent actor, for he showed not the slightest perturbation. Skilful as Hatfield was in reading and judging men, he could not pick out anything suspicious in Barstowe's bearing.

"Yes, sir, he did," Barstowe answered him, and nodded genially. "I understood that he'd written to Austin, asking for help against the rustlers. Of course I'm in entire sympathy with this, and with you, Ranger Hatfield. You must call on me if there's anything I can do to be of service."

"I worked in at Carns' hide-out the other day," drawled Hatfield, watching Barstowe closely, "and I was gettin' on fine with 'em till a warning note was brought in describin' me as a Ranger. The only man I told here was Fenton — and he told you."

Barstowe looked troubled, but any decent person might have been in trying to understand the significance of that remark.

"Well, surely you can't believe that Fenton or I would have sent such a communication to the rustlers," Barstowe said.

Hatfield shrugged. He decided that Fenton must be right, that a spy had seen him and figured out who he was, or else had overheard Fenton explaining to Barstowe about him.

The banker reached for the glass at his hand. He had suddenly realized that he had not offered a drink to his guest.

"Excuse me — please have a drink." He reached behind him and from the cabinet took down a decanter. It had a red diamond label on it. "This is the finest Napoleon brandy," he assured. "I reserve it for special occasions."

His smile was benevolent and his hand steady as he poured the golden liquid into a clean, thin-stemmed glass. He handed the drink to the Ranger, who raised it to his lips.

Across the top of the fine glass Hatfield could read one of the framed mottoes which adorned the walls:

There's Many a Slip 'Twixt Cup & Lip!

Hatfield started slightly as he heard a faint sound from somewhere, and he set the glass down on Barstowe's desk. His glance flicked to the open window behind him, for he was on guard with Pecos Carns and his powerful gang on the hunt for him.

The sound which had startled him, however, had come from the other door, which led into the hallway, and to Fenton's office.

"What's wrong?" demanded Barstowe.

"Someone's in the hall."

Hatfield stood up, slim hands hanging ready at his hips, where his loaded Colts reposed in their oiled holsters.

Then the steps were louder, and the door opened on John Fenton and another man in range clothing — brown whipcord pants tucked into black boots, a blue shirt, bandanna and Stetson. Fenton's companion was a slight fellow of about forty-five, whose dark hair was just touched by gray at the temples. He had a keen, fine face, and in his brown eyes was the steady gaze of honesty.

"Oh — sorry to horn in, gents," Fenton apologized, seeing the tall Ranger in Barstowe's office. "I wanted to have a word with you, Barstowe, about Whittemore here. He says he lost most of his cows yestiddy. He trailed 'em south for ten miles, and he figgers there was eight rustlers drivin' 'em hard for the Border. It was a part of Pecos Carns' gang, no doubt."

"Sorry to hear that," murmured Barstowe, but his eyes were on Hatfield.

Fred Whittemore, one of the small ranchers of the new development, stepped forward.

"Unless we can get back them cattle, Mr. Barstowe, I'm hard hit. I owe you three hundred and yuh got my note to call when yuh want. Fact is, I promised to pay yuh somethin' today."

Barstowe waved his pudgy hand. The odor of brandy and of the perfume of hair tonic the broker liked mingled in the warm office air.

"Don't let it worry you, Whittemore," he said in a kindly tone. "We'll work something out. It's distressing, though. These cattle thieves must be checked. Of course, I have commitments in other places which I must meet, but we'll work it out, one way or another."

Whittemore was painfully anxious and worried.

"I wouldn't want to put on you, Mr. Barstowe," he mumbled. "Not after yuh've been so good to us all."

Fenton, too, was worried. "We've got to give Fred more time, Barstowe," he said flatly. "He's got five kids, and his wife ain't been so well lately."

"Of course — of course," said Barstowe. "We'll work it out all right."

Chapter IX
Loaded with Death

Hatfield had stepped near the side window as Whittemore and Fenton had come to Barstowe's desk. He glanced out, as he listened to the talk between the men. He could see westward for a long distance, though the dropping sun was reddening, and bright in his eyes.

As he idly stared, suddenly he saw something that glinted. Then riders emerged from the direct path of the sun, and at their head he recognized Pecos Carns' big figure on a black stallion. Fifteen to twenty of his men were strung out behind the red-haired leader.

One of them got down, and examined the trail into Fentonville. The rest waited, and when their companion remounted they resumed their run, straight toward the settlement.

"Trackin' Goldy, a thousand to one!" decided the Ranger, tense as he watched.

Barstowe must have noticed his attitude, for he called:

"What's wrong, sir?"

"Fenton — Pecos Carns is here!" shouted Hatfield. "Get organized!"

Goldy stood in the yard, and as the advancing riders came close enough to see the gelding, Carns raised an arm and pointed. The rustlers picked up speed, headed for Barstowe's office. Hatfield went out the back window and ran for his horse.

John Fenton and his rancher friend, Whittemore, hurried to the window. As Hatfield threw a shot to slow them up, Fenton opened fire on Carns and his gang. The outlaws answered, their lead rapping into the side of the building. They saw the tall Ranger in the saddle, gun in hand, on the golden gelding they had been trailing. Hatfield knew that such experts could have identified the sorrel's hoofprints back at the hide-out and then picked them up on the range trails. They whooped in triumph as they spurred and quirted, racing their mounts forward.

Blasts of six-gun and carbine fire held Fenton and Whittemore crouched down inside the window. The horsemen swerved out, on Hatfield's trail, as the Ranger, seeking to protect those in the settlement, raced away toward the Pecos.

Quickly pursued and pursuers were past the buildings. Fenton and other men ran outside, to shoot after the outlaws, but they were traveling in risen dust, and out of Colt range.

Hot after the Ranger, Pecos Carns rode furiously. Such men hated all Rangers, who brought them to book. Here was a chance to get even, and Carns had plenty of assistance. It was eighteen to one, as they flogged after him.

Now and then one would raise a carbine and try for Hatfield, but the jolting of the man's horse, the flying speed of the chase, prevented exact aim. Hatfield, low over the gelding, heard the whistling lead, but it was wide.

Pecos Carns pressed eagerly after him. Hatfield waited, holding his fire, hoping that the rustler chief might get out ahead of his men. But Carns was crafty. He had seen a sample of Hatfield's gun speed, and did not intend to take too many chances with his own life.

Fortunately Goldy was rested, there was nothing for Hatfield to do but outride the bloodthirsty gang.

Ahead lay the deep canyon of the Pecos, and the Ranger could not afford to be stopped in his tracks. He swerved gradually to the north, so the men after him could not shortcut and get closer.

He traveled for a mile parallel with the river canyon but, aware that a side creek would block him, he worked westward, and the sorrel galloped into the setting sun. Several of the rustlers, on inferior mounts, had fallen behind in the race, but Carns and ten of his men were still at it.

"Figger if they can finish me off, before I report, they'll have more time," the Ranger thought grimly.

They had passed north of the settlement, which now lay in the distance. Goldy was damp with lather but his breathing was excellent, for Hatfield had not let him out altogether. The fierce rustlers came a quarter-mile behind.

Now the fiery red ball that was the sun dropped behind the mountains of the Trans-Pecos, and the land was plunged into a purple light. Darkness came, stars and rising moon appeared.

The pursuing owlhoots held on for another hour, but though the pace had slowed, they could no longer see him. Patches of black brush, stunted woods, and rock formations, hid the Ranger. He had led them in a wide circle and when he pulled up, to listen for sounds of the pursuit, he could not hear the mustang hoofs of the gang.

"Sort of got discouraged," he decided wryly.

He walked Goldy to a height and sat his saddle peering across the moonlit plain. But Pecos Carns and his men had given up the run.

In the northeast distance, yellow lights blinked in the night — Fentonville. And Hatfield also could see distant lights at three of the ranches west of town, among them John Fenton's place. In each little spot human beings lived, with the hopes and troubles of all mankind. Black danger hung over this range, and the Ranger, alone, must defeat the powerful forces aligned against them.

"Now I wonder what Carns'll do next?" he muttered. "I reckon I'll sashay back to the town and poke around there."

He moved cautiously, and approached Fentonville, always alert for any signs of his foes. The lights were going out in the settlement for people there turned in early. The saloon was still open, but Fenton's and Barstowe's offices were dark.

Around ten o'clock, the stealthy Ranger, leaving his horse hidden in the brush out from the town, silently crept in to reconnoiter. Pecos Carns, with his gang, could take over such a small place if he so desired.

But Fentonville was quiet in the night. A couple of lights still burned in small cabins. He peeked through a side window into the saloon. The drinking oasis was empty, except for the bartender who was dozing in a chair. Even Old Pete had left.

Hatfield made his way to the end of the settlement, staying in Tin Can Alley, behind the row of buildings so the shadows hid him. At the back of Barstowe's office a window was open, and Hatfield paused to check up. There was no light anywhere in the place, either in the Central Pecos Development Company's quarters, or in Barstowe's.

As he listened, crouched at one side of the open window, he heard strange sounds from Barstowe's office, sounds he could not identify. The noises puzzled him.

"Sounds like a man chokin' to death, and kickin' his heels on the floor!" he decided at last.

A logical explanation occurred to him.

"Mebbe Carns robbed Barstowe and left him gagged and tied up!"

A gag would account for the awful gasps the Ranger heard, and a victim of a holdup, lying trussed on the floor, would kick with his heels. Something made of glass rolled, and tinkled in the room beyond the open window.

Hatfield felt called upon to investigate. He drew a Colt and held the hammer spur back under his thumb, ready to shoot, as he thrust a leg over the sill and quickly entered by the window.

No shot came at him. He stood away from the window through which he had come, seeking to focus his eyes in the darkness. Queer soft sounds came from the direction of the desk. The Ranger began to move that way, making no noise as he tiptoed across the office.

The chokings were awful, inhuman. The thumpings had grown weaker.

He could see better now, as his pupils accustomed themselves to the dimness. He could make out the shapes of chairs, of the desk. Pale moonlight streaming in the front windows glinted on the glass of Barstowe's liquor cabinet.

A dark bulk lay on the mat in front of the broker's desk.

Hatfield stooped, believing for a moment that his guess had been right, that the outlaws had come in to steal and had left a victim trussed on the floor. His slim, searching hand touched clothing, and he realized that the body inside it was arched, and stiff as a board. But the hands were not secured, nor the feet. The Ranger's fingers paused for an instant on the bearded face. There was no gag.

Puzzled, he took hold of the man as the body relaxed. He turned him over, trying to see the fellow's face in the moonlight. As he moved him, another convulsion seized the prostrate victim. He flexed back on his head and heels, back arched, and his teeth gritted violently. His breath was a horrible rasp, but as the Ranger sought to help him, it stopped. The body stayed stiff, however, in his arms.

It was horrible, there in the darkness, with a man who had just died. Curiosity, pity, swept the Ranger. He lighted a match, keeping it shaded by the palm of his hand.

By the faint illumination as it flared, he recognized Old Pete, the town drunkard and loafer. He knew the ragged clothing, the bearded features, though they were ghastly, drawn, the eyes rolled back till only the whites showed. Old Pete was dead now, and his tongue stuck from his bluish lips.

"What the —"

Hatfield lit another match, hunting

around the floor. A decanter lay half under the desk. It bore a red diamond label on its round side. It was empty. Hatfield concluded that Old Pete had drunk the contents.

The liquor cupboard had been pried open with Old Pete's knife. The drunkard had broken in, stolen Barstowe's brandy.

The Ranger sniffed at the mouth of the flask from which Old Pete had obviously drunk deep. He tried another match, to examine it. Then he could see some tiny white crystals, not dissolved in the bottom of the flask.

The convulsions, the symptoms, told that Old Pete had just died from the poison which the Ranger recognized by its color.

"Strychnine!" he growled.

His nostrils dilated, and his flesh prickled. That decanter of "fine old Napoleon brandy" had been loaded with death!

"Why, I dang near took a drink of it myself this afternoon!" he thought. "Barstowe offered it to me!" Squatted there, he hunted back through his mind, turning over and over the details he had learned since he had come to Fentonville. "And George Tate, that little Emily girl's dad, he died of strychnine poisonin' — s'posed to have taken it hisself. Now, I wonder!"

The first faint suspicion he had had about Barstowe flamed high.

"The old devil! He's got a mighty pious look, and he poses as a philanthropist. What's he doin' with poison likker in his office? I'll give a thousand to one now he's hooked up with Pecos Carns. He was the one sent that warnin' to the rustlers that near finished me."

Determinedly he straightened up. He hunted around, and found a piece of candle in one of the desk drawers. He lighted it, seeking to keep it shaded with a piece of stiff paper he made into a shield. In a corner stood a file, and he squatted in front of it and began to examine the records in the drawers. He had to break the lock to get at them, but he felt justified.

There were records of loans here, to such ranchers as John Fenton, George Tate, Fred Whittemore, Arthur Simsbury, and others of the district. Demand notes and, worse still for those to whom Barstowe had lent sums of money, were quit-claim deeds, signed and attested. Stock certificates, too, in big denominations on the Central Pecos Development Company. The enormity of Barstowe's scheme almost took away the Ranger's breath.

"The dirty cuss has 'em in his paw, any time he wants to close it!" he muttered. "He's a philanthropist, all right — only for hisself!"

He thought deeply, seeking some way by which he could frustrate Silas Barstowe. Fenton, Whittemore, the rest of the settlers were decent Texans, but they were inexperienced in legal affairs and in protecting themselves from such a thief as Barstowe, who had used John Fenton as a figurehead to bring in the dupes. They were the kind of men whose word was their bond. A contract didn't need to be written to hold with them. They had believed in Barstowe and had done as he instructed them.

"If these records should get burned up, it'd save a lot of tribulation," he mused. "That idea ain't legal, mebbe, but neither is Barstowe."

The Ranger was not expecting what happened then — a bullet that threw splinters into his face. He heard the crashing explosion of the gun at the window, and dived for the Colt he had laid on the floor as he had examined Barstowe's records.

Chapter X

Mounting Threats

With fighting fury in his heart, Hatfield got off a shot which tore through the open window. His second one, fired while he paused in his rolling motion on the floor, cut a groove in the sill at the side. He had glimpsed a black Colt muzzle pointed at him, held by someone who had crept up to the window. He was rolling for the protection of the desk as the blue-yellow stab of his heavy revolver once more pierced the night.

As the explosions banged back and forth in Barstowe's office, Hatfield's ears rang with the sounds. He got to the desk and still crouched, steadied himself with his left hand on the ledge of it as he faced the window outside of which was someone who had sought to kill him.

But no more shots came through the window. And as the sounds of his own shooting died off, he heard swift-running footsteps in the alley.

He jumped up, rushed to the window. After a quick look he went out through it. Whoever it was had turned between buildings and was not in his range of vision. He ran along the other side of the square building where Barstowe had his offices, and paused at the road, hunting for his attacker with his eyes.

After a time he caught a shadowy movement to the right, up the line and across the dirt main street. It was a horseman, on his way out of town. Hatfield ran toward him, but the range was long for a pistol and the rider passed behind the structures west of the settlement untouched.

From the saloon door, the bartender, alarmed at the shooting, sang out:

"Hey, you! You doin' that gunnin'? Come here before I give yuh a taste of this buckshot!"

He had a shotgun leveled and could see Hatfield plainly in the road.

"It's all right, feller," called Hatfield, turning toward him. "Hold yore fire. I'm after a bandit!"

It took a couple of minutes to satisfy the bartender with a logical explanation. When he had accomplished this, Hatfield inquired:

"Where does Silas Barstowe live?"

"See that third house over there, the one with the light in front?" said the barkeep. "That's his'n."

Hatfield hurried across the street. The front door of Barstowe's home stood ajar, and a lamp burned low on a round table in the front room. Some newspapers, books, a box of cigars, a decanter of brandy, and three dirty glasses stood on the table. A cheroot still smouldered in an ash receiver, and a couple of cold cigar butts also were in the tray.

Someone with muddy boots had sat in one of the chairs, facing Barstowe's armchair, but the two-room house was empty.

Hatfield searched the place. All he found was food in the rear room, a small stove, and various belongings such as clothing, toilet articles and other personal things.

"Barstowe tried for me again," he mused, when finally he stepped out the rear door and stared across the moonlit plain west of the settlement. "I'll get back to his office and take charge of that file."

Pounding hoofs, rapidly approaching, drew his attention. They increased in volume as a number of riders came toward Fentonville. The Ranger waited, his hammer spur back under a long thumb.

"Wonder how far Pecos Carns was from

Fentonville!" came to his mind. "Mebbe Barstowe caught up with him already and is fetchin' him back. I reckon it was Carns who smoked one of them cigars and had a drink at Barstowe's this evenin', after he lost me in the monte!"

He faded back, to pick up Goldy. His hunch was right. He saw a band of fifteen men enter the town, and hurry to Barstowe's office. They searched up and down the street, and inside the building, then went into the saloon and questioned the bartender. From a distance, Hatfield could see them in the lights, and hear their rough voices. It was Pecos Carns and his gang, as he had surmised.

A couple of the outlaws rode away after a time, but the rest remained. Hatfield checked up, when they had quieted, and saw that their horses had been unsaddled, and were being held under guard behind Barstowe's business place. Carns had come to town, probably to take over.

"Looks like they mean to stay for a while, this time," decided the Ranger.

Barstowe was aware now of what the Texas Ranger had learned about him and his vicious scheme. The investment man knew his danger.

"He ain't the sort to run and leave all

this gravy, though," concluded Hatfield, as he figured out what the man's next move might be. "He's goin' to hit, and fight to hold what he's got. He has a close connection with Pecos Carns and he means to use the rustlers as strong-arm men."

He turned the sorrel and started away from the settlement. It was in enemy hands.

"I'll hustle out and warn Fenton," he decided. "The show-down ain't far off now."

It was near midnight when he approached Fenton's. The house stood dark against the sky. Hatfield dropped Goldy's reins in the side yard and went to the back door. As he was about to knock, a voice said:

"Who's that this time of night!"

It was John Fenton. Restless, again unable to sleep because of his lost son Nat, the rancher had been sitting up in the window and had seen the shadowy horseman.

"It's Hatfield, Fenton," the Ranger answered in a subdued voice. "Get on yore duds and come out. I want to talk with yuh. Don't like to disturb folks at such an hour but it's life and death."

It wasn't long before Fenton joined him, and they went to the barn where they could talk without rousing those in the house.

"I've had a big time, Fenton," began the

Ranger. "I got to tell yuh that Silas Barstowe is as mean an Injun as ever come down the pike. He's used you and yore name to develop this district, and now he's in cahoots with Pecos Carns. After havin' had you folks build up these properties, he's takin' over and sellin' 'em at a big profit. All that sweetness and light he pours out is so much makeup, like an actor wears."

"I — I can't believe it!" Fenton gasped. His eyes gleamed in the faint light.

"You will, and pronto," the Ranger promised. "Barstowe's scared now. He already savvied I'm a Ranger and now he knows I'm on to his game, and he'll have to hit fast and hard. He needs time to cash in on his scheme, which is to sell yore improved properties to other folks with money to pay him. There's a fortune in it for him. I seen Barstowe's records. He's got notes, and quit-claim deeds from you fellers. Why'd yuh sign such deeds? Yuh put yoreselves in his power."

"We — we trusted him like a brother!" Fenton said weakly. "I guaranteed him to my friends, the folks I brought out here. Most of the boys thought they were signin' notes for the money he lent — I know I did. Barstowe said it was just a formality!"

"Yeah, I s'pose he tricked yuh, but he's got yore signatures. It's legal enough, as far as the Development Company goes. But Fenton, a confidence man is the meanest kind of thief, the way he lies and fools people. Barstowe's nose ain't clean on other matters, either. I've got reason to believe he fed strychnine to yore friend George Tate, in poison brandy. He near got me with it, and this evenin' Old Pete, the tramp, busted in there and died from the stuff."

"Why would he kill Tate?"

Hatfield shrugged. "Mebbe when he told Tate the bad news, Tate kicked up such a fuss Barstowe figgered he'd get rid of him. Was Tate the sort who'd take loss of his ranch lyin' down?"

"No, he wasn't. Some of 'em might, if they thought it was legal, but Tate loved his spread." Fenton added slowly, "I reckon what yuh say is right, Ranger." His voice was faint. He hung his head, his fists clenched. "It's all my fault, this trouble," he declared. "I brought 'em all in here."

"Barstowe tricked yuh, used yuh for a figgerhead. We got to fight back, Fenton. Mebbe we can beat Barstowe and save somethin' from the wreck."

Fenton raised his head. Anger was fast

mounting in his heart against the perfidious Barstowe.

"I'm goin' to saddle up right now and go after him!" he growled. "He'll turn over them deeds or I'll gun him!"

"Yuh'll be shot for yore pains," drawled the Ranger. "Pecos Carns and his bunch are in town — looks like they're there to take over."

Hatfield turned, with a warning touch on Fenton's arm. He had caught the sound of approaching hoofs. Hurrying to the end of the barn, he looked across the flat toward Fentonville. He could make out several riders heading toward them.

"I think some of 'em are here!" he rasped. "Let's get inside the house pronto, Fenton. They may be hittin' yuh already."

They ran to the kitchen, Hatfield pausing on the way to pick up Goldy's reins and send the sorrel running off, free, so that he might keep out of the way of flying lead. Inside the house, they waited, one at either side of the east kitchen window, looking out at the yard. Before long the horsemen came up quietly.

Three dismounted. Hatfield saw the glint of the moonlight on rifle barrels.

"Challenge 'em," ordered Hatfield in a whisper.

"Halt, there!" sang out Fenton, a cocked carbine in his hands resting on the sill.

They stopped, hunting for the source of the voice. One man in the rear, near the barn, said in a voice which rasped like a dull saw in hard wood:

"That you, Fenton?"

"That's Pecos Carns hisself," murmured Hatfield. He knew the rustler's voice. "Go on, answer him."

"Yeah, it's me — John Fenton. This is my ranch."

"Yuh mean it was yore ranch," growled Carns. "It ain't now. We got a deed signin' it over. See this badge I'm wearin'? I'm a special marshal who's takin' over this property in the name of the rightful owner."

"Yuh dirty rustler!" shouted Fenton, his temper snapping. "I ought to gun yuh! You and yore killer shot my boy Nat. Yuh'll pay the piper for it, I guarantee that!"

"Take it easy, Fenton," warned the Ranger. "No use to go off half-cocked."

The boys, Jack Fenton and Sam Tate, and the women were awakening in the house as the loud voices called back and forth. Pecos Carns, "King of the Rustlers", replied to Fenton's threat after a moment.

"Yuh old goat," he said contemptuously. "I savvy yuh. And I'll take care of yuh any

116

time. Yuh got till dark tomorrer to git out of here, the whole passel of you squatters. If yuh're around when I come agin, yuh'll stay here — under the grass. This is the first and last warnin'."

Carns turned his horse, and rode off. His men quickly followed. There were but half a dozen of them in the band that had come to Fenton's, and they did not fancy a charge at the darkened house, with guns trained on them from the windows. Anyway, thought the Ranger, they no doubt had other places to visit, and had split their forces to give the warnings that were to frighten out the ranchers. "They'll come a-shootin' tomorrer night, the entire gang, I reckon," he thought angrily.

Chapter XI
Safety Problem

Before long the women and the boys in the Fenton ranch-house had been calmed down. But hardly had they been reassured that Carns and his outlaws were gone when Fred Whittemore galloped into the yard and threw himself from his lathered horse. The rancher, Fenton's friend and neighbor, was breathless as he came into the kitchen that was lighted by an oil lamp.

"John!" he shouted. "Passel of tough hombres stopped at my house a while ago and threatened to kill me if I wasn't gone by tomorrer night! They said my ranch had been sold to somebody else. They had a deed, they claimed! Mebbe so, but Barstowe sort of promised to give me more time."

"Set down, Fred," Fenton said quietly.

He bit his lip, then tried to tell his friend of Barstowe's perfidy. Hatfield broke in, to help him.

"Barstowe's a first class confidence man,

Whittemore. He's got yuh legal-like, and he's goin' to run yuh all off by usin' Pecos Carns and his men as strong-arm 'deputies'. It ain't Fenton's fault. He was took in like all of yuh."

"I'm mighty sorry, Fred," said Fenton. "I keep blamin' myself. But mebbe we can fight Barstowe down, with the Ranger's help."

Whittemore stared from Fenton to the tall man on whose vest now shone a silver star on silver circle, emblem of the mighty Texas Rangers.

"So yuh're a Ranger," he said. "Well, I'm mighty glad yuh're with us." He looked back at Fenton, then put a hand on the rancher's shoulder. "Don't take it so hard, John. Yuh're all right with me, no matter what. If Barstowe fooled you, he did all of us."

Fenton raised his head. A brighter light came into his eyes. He sighed deeply.

"Yore friends'll stick by yuh, Fenton," the Ranger said softly.

"We'll fight, shore as we live and breathe!" declared Whittemore.

When he understood the details of Barstowe's treachery, Whittemore asked:

"How about the women and kids? We can't let Carns and his killers touch 'em.

119

That's all I'm a-feared of."

"Yuh'll have to band together, and pronto," said Hatfield, taking command. "By this time, Carns or his men have visited all the ranches and give the folks till tomorrer night to vacate, I'll guarantee that. Whittemore, you go on back home, pack yore folks and what valuables yuh can carry in a wagon, and come back here. Yuh pass near any neighbor on yore way?"

Whittemore's route home took him close to the outfit of another rancher, Ed Porter. He would give Porter the Ranger's instructions. Jack Jr., young Sam Tate, and Fenton saddled up, and hurried off in different directions, to carry the warning to all the settlers. Hatfield remained at Fenton's to rest himself and Goldy, and to think out his next step.

"This place ain't big enough to hold all these folks," he mused. "Ain't food for 'em all either, for any length of time."

They might have to hold out for some time, too, against Pecos Carns' hard-shooting rustlers. There had been around thirty of the owlhoots at the creek canyon hideout, but Hatfield knew that Carns had had other men out working at the time. When they all assembled, Pecos Carns would be able to muster fifty fighters or more. They would make a formidable force, particularly since the cowmen had women and children to protect.

"Sort of ties our hands that this place ain't made for easy defense," he thought.

The house walls were thin, and the barn was no fortress. They would all need food, and a spot where a few men could be left to protect the families, while the others went out to attack the killers.

The grayness of the new day was stealing over the range when Fred Whittemore came back, driving a flat wagon loaded with his family and movable possessions. They had no illusions about Carns' men. They knew the outlaws would loot their homes. Whittemore had a young wife and several growing children, and his parents had come to the Trans-Pecos to share the new life that had begun so hopefully.

As the sun came up, reddening the sky, Ed Porter drove in with his wife and children stowed in his wagon. Others arrived as the morning passed. Fenton, Jack, and Sam returned, having given warnings to all their friends.

Everyone shook hands with the tall Ranger whose appearance heartened them. All had been told of Barstowe's thievery and cruelty, of the danger which beset them.

Mrs. Fenton, Em Tate, and the other women got breakfast ready, and men, women and children were fed. Then Hatfield called the men together, taking them to the barnyard to confer.

They were sturdy people, most of them of little means. This land had been their great hope in life where they had planned to make homes in the new country across the Pecos. Now the hopes were dashed. But taking their place was a rising faith in the serene, powerful Hatfield who had come to help them.

As he took stock of his fighting forces, the Ranger hid the doubts he felt as to how much they might accomplish. There was no time to send out for help. Before such assistance could be reached, collected and brought to bear on Barstowe, many here would be dead, and the rest scattered.

There were some thirty men in the gathering capable of bearing arms — fathers of families, their older sons, and a sprinkling of oldsters. In numbers, led by the towering Ranger, they might have a chance against Carns at two-to-one odds.

But he soon found that they were short of ammunition. They had had no large stores of it, for they were peaceful, using their guns only to protect themselves from marauding beasts, or to hunt game.

They had always been able before this to buy more at the Fentonville store, but it was closed to them now, since Barstowe and Carns held the town. Hatfield, who had lost his own gear at Carns' hide-out, had only Colts, and no reserve.

The same situation faced them where food was concerned but they had enough on Fenton's ranch to feed such a large gathering for a short time, though some more had been brought in the wagons.

"Boys," the Ranger said soberly, "one thing's certain — we can't stick here. There ain't room enough to shelter us all proper-like, and we need ammunition. Nearest town, outside of Fenton, which they've took over, is a hundred miles off, and it ain't too big. There's just one place I figger'll hold us all, and where we can find the guns and such we must have pronto."

"Where's that?" demanded Fenton.

"Over at Pecos Carns' place."

They stared at him, chins dropped in astonishment.

"Yuh mean the rustler hide-out in the crik canyon?" inquired John Fenton at last.

"That's it."

"But how yuh figger on gettin' in there?"

"I savvy just where it lies. I've been

there. And Pecos Carns has made a mistake in strategy. I reckon he's left only a skeleton force to hold his stronghold. Carns and his main gang are in Fentonville with Barstowe. They've left their base wide open to attack!"

Whittemore whistled, then a grin spread over his face.

"Shucks I believe yuh're right, Ranger! If we can take it —"

"— we'll have plenty food, guns, bullets, horses, and it's as good as a fort, held right. I've figgered out a way to capture it. Get yore families loaded up, and we'll start, before Carns and his gang are on the prowl."

The Ranger's plan was at once so bold, so simple, that it enthused the ranchers. Hurriedly they began to carry out his orders.

"I'm takin' a run over toward the settlement," Hatfield told Fenton, after he had called Goldy and saddled the sorrel.

One of the ranchers lent him a field-glass and he rode off, picking up speed as he galloped across the golden range for Fentonville. From a height, from which he could survey the town, he trained his glass on the town, simply checking up on Carns.

He saw men, Carns' followers, on the

road, their mustangs grazing under guard nearby. The saloon was doing a land-office business, and the general store, too, had plenty of customers as the hungry rustlers took over.

He recognized the tall, raw-boned figure of Pecos Carns when the King of the Rustlers emerged from the saloon, wiping his mouth on his sleeve, and stalked to Barstowe's office. The Ranger counted forty outlaws in sight. They had taken over the town, lock, stock and barrel all right.

When he got back to Fenton's ranch, the people there were ready to start. Hatfield led them northwest toward rising rough hills and the creek canyon. He knew the way, the hidden trails. His chief anxiety was that Carns and his main gang might, for some reason, decide to pay a visit to their hide-out before he could make his play. But they planned to take over the ranches that evening, and he figured they would remain in Fentonville until that time.

Reaching the entrance to the blind in-trail, it was necessary to desert the wheeled vehicles. Wagons could not negotiate that narrow, tortuous way. Hatfield gave orders for the women and children to be hidden in a grassy dell in the chaparral and left a few men to stand guard over them. He gave final orders to John Fenton, and, with three young men, left the main party and pushed into dense, thorned bush which lay south of the creek ravine.

It was hard going. They had to cut a path sometimes, and their leather was scratched, their flesh torn by the sharp thorns of the chaparral. Each man carried two lariats over his shoulders.

From the tall officer's previous visit to Carns' hide-out, he knew where it lay. And he could pick out the conical tops of a clump of three tall spruce trees, arranged in a peculiar pattern, which marked the upper rim of the canyon not far from the buildings which were hidden on the lower shelves of the rock.

Toward these they forged, fighting the sullen brush.

The sun was blazing hot, the air ovenlike and stuffy, when the Ranger crept to the edge of the first steep drop and peeked down into the deep canyon, choked with trees and brush. He could not see any of the buildings below for projecting rock strata, and tangled growth which had found foothold on the more horizontal sections of the walls cut off the view.

But across the ravine stood the three tall

black spruce trees. And they were perhaps three hundred yards down the canyon toward the Pecos, from the house.

Hatfield signaled to Jack Fenton, one of the three whom he had brought along to serve as aides.

"Tie yore lariat to the trunk of that big oak, Jack," he ordered. "I'll go down first, then the rest of yuh come one at a time, when I signal."

"Shore, Ranger!"

Young Sam Tate, thrilled by the dangerous work, and Ed Porter's eldest son, Barney, were eager for the descent.

Hatfield checked the knots, then let himself over the first drop, about twelve feet to a ledge which was wide enough to hold several small trees and brush. He watched his step for there would be plenty of rattlesnakes on these ledges.

But the sun was hot and the reptiles preferred the shade in such weather.

He saw splits in the face of the grayish rock, no doubt marking dens, as the forty-foot lariat let him easily down a slanting, sandy slope to the next drop. He fastened another lariat to a well-rooted pine tree there, and turned to signal to the boys. They were athletic youngsters, trained to riding and climbing. Such work was easy for them. With their carbines strapped to backs, they soon stood beside the officer as he reconnoitered, crouched on the lower shelf. He could see the opposite bank of the canyon, but not yet the buildings housing the rustlers.

Hatfield's practised eye could read the time, almost to the minute, by the sun's course, but to be sure he checked with Jack Fenton's turnip watch which had been set with his father's.

It was 1:33 and they had almost half an hour before John Fenton and his attackers would strike.

Chapter XII

Stronghold

Making sure of knots, and on hand to help in case one of the youths slipped, Hatfield cautiously worked his way down into the ravine, ledge by ledge. Twice they heard the ominous whirrings of big rattlers, coiled under bushes, for the reptiles would die in the direct rays of the summer sun. Given warning, however, they were able to avoid the snakes, and at last the Ranger, with the boys crouched behind him, was able to see the front of Carns' roof.

"Two o'clock, Jim!" Jack whispered hoarsely.

"Get yore carbines ready," ordered Hatfield, "and don't run ahead of me, now. Do as I do."

They were a couple of hundred yards down from the main hide-out, with some brush screening them. Listening intently, they regained their breath.

It was several minutes before gunfire opened, violently, up the canyon at the narrows. The young men lifted their heads alertly, looking eagerly at Hatfield for orders.

"Hold yore hosses," he warned. "Give 'em a chance to run up there."

His young aides were straining at the leash. Such youths were wonderful, thought the Ranger. They were so eager, so easily taught and molded. Anything could be done with them. They never tired, could go long hours without food and sleep, fighting constantly, and bounce back after a nap, to fight on.

They had a capacity for hero worship which was tremendous, and they had chosen the Texas Ranger to look to. They were immensely flattered that he had picked them to go along with him, and each sought to imitate his manner, his expression.

It had not been long, mused the Ranger, when he himself had been just such an eager, green youth. Now he was an experienced, hardened fighting man. But he realized that he must be careful of his actions, for anything he did would be picked up and considered right by the lads.

Some hoarse shouts, heard above the increasing gunfire, rang echoing in the creek canyon. A woman screamed.

"Filly!" thought Hatfield.

He nodded to the young fellows. They came after him as he slid down a sloping bank and landed on his feet, pantherlike, on the rough path.

With his aides at his heels, Hatfield ran lightly toward the house. He stared at it eagerly. There was only one man in sight — the stout Brownie of the round head and stringy brown hair. Brownie was looking up the ravine, toward the sounds of battle there. The rest of the home guard had rushed to the narrows to protect the stronghold.

It was working out as Hatfield had figured — and hoped. Pecos Carns had pulled out his main forces, to carry out Barstowe's schemes. Counting on the inaccessibility of the stronghold, and that no one was aware of its exact location, he had left only a skeleton crew.

Hatfield was within a hundred feet of Brownie before the outlaw heard a stone clack under one of the feet of the running boys. He glanced around, and his horrified eyes were like moons as he recognized who was upon him.

"Throw down, Brownie!" shouted Hatfield.

The sun slanting into the canyon

touched the silver star on silver circle. Brownie knew who this man was, anyway, because of the warning from Barstowe that had come to Pecos Carns.

The stout rustler gave a squeal of fear. He had a sawed-off shotgun in his blunt hands. From its two barrels murderous buckshot would pour, spread, and perhaps injure or kill one of the youths with the Ranger, if not Hatfield himself.

Before the stout outlaw could fire, however, Hatfield got off a pistol shot. Brownie let go of the shotgun, yipping with agony. He doubled over, gripping his punctured shoulder with his hand.

As Hatfield paused, to check Brownie, a bullet whirled past his ear. Sam Tate and Barney Porter quickly threw up their carbines and almost simultaneously fired at the window from which the shot had come.

A panic-stricken feminine shriek reached the Ranger.

"Take it easy, boys," he ordered. "Work up close under the foundations till I go inside."

He rushed the side door and, guns up, jumped into the main room. As he had thought, it was Filly, Carns' girl, who had fired from the window, but the whistling lead about her ears had sent her reeling back. She lay in a heap on the floor sobbing, shrinking from him, the pearl-handled Colt she had used near her hand.

"Filly, yuh little fool, yuh near got it that time," growled the Ranger. "Go on into yore room and behave yoreself before yuh get hurt."

The girl wept. She seized his knees, pleading:

"Don't kill me — please don't! Oh, where's Pecos? Where's my baby boy!"

"He's off on business right now," the Ranger said dryly. "If yuh want some good advice, Filly, yuh'll forget that red-headed side-winder and go on home and try to be a decent girl."

She pulled herself together, as she realized the gentleness of the big man toward a woman. Her bold eyes sought his, as she stood up, and faced him.

"You're nice," she said softly. "I — I wish I'd of never taken up with Carns."

Hatfield checked her obvious advances, took her arm, and steered her toward her room.

"Stick there, Filly, and I'll see yuh ain't hurt. Don't try any more drygulchin'. The jig's up."

He had dangerous work to do. He hurried out, signaled to the three youths, and started toward the narrows.

Keeping them behind him, the Ranger swung past the last obstacle before the huge, looming rock shoulder which held the narrows. Disposed here, in perfect cover, were seven of the rustlers. They were shooting from their shelters. Around the turn the men under John Fenton were keeping them occupied.

Hatfield signaled to his aides to take cover. His guns rose, toward the enemy rear.

"Throw down!" he bellowed, his stentorian tones carrying over the crackling of the carbines.

A rustler looked back, then another. They saw the tall officer with his Colts up. One whirled to fire, but a .45 slug bit into his body. He slumped, his rifle clattering in the rocks.

"Come on, Fenton!" shouted Hatfield at the top of his voice.

Blasts of guns rose, and John Fenton, leading his settlers, charged the gap. Hatfield's Colts insured them, and in a minute Fenton and his followers were in. The outlaws knew who and what the tall Ranger was. Sick with fear, beaten, the handful of Carns' men put down their weapons, and raised their hands high.

Fenton smiled as he gripped the Ranger's hand, after his first anxious glance to see that Jack Jr. and the other youths were safe and sound.

"Yuh done it, Ranger! That was mighty fine work!"

"Let's fetch in the women and kids," ordered Hatfield. "Send some of yore men back for 'em. We want to be set here before night."

A contingent started back to lead the rest of the settlers into the outlaw stronghold.

Hatfield had hustled up the ravine, to help Fenton through the pass. Now he returned to the house, for he had not had time to search it thoroughly. Brownie was still there, nursing his wounded shoulder, leaning against the house foundation and holding his arm. Filly, too, was in her room.

But down the canyon, the Ranger saw a slight figure turn the corner, hurrying toward the Pecos — a woman, one of the squaws who had served the rustlers at the hide-out.

"Sam — Jack," he sang out. They hurried to him, and he pointed down the ravine. "See if yuh can catch her. She's goin' to carry the alarm to Carns!"

Fleet of foot, the boys ran down the path toward the river.

Fenton and some of his men were coming through the front door. Hatfield went to look around back, to make sure no more enemies were hiding in the various shacks. As he passed the spot where the chain showed, an animal-like growl startled him. Then he remembered the unfortunate man whom Carns had kept to bedevil.

He was chained, and he had drawn himself up into the kennel-like recess where he slept, a couple of horse blankets for his bed. The remains of meals, gnawed bones and crusts of bread, lay about.

"Come out, feller," the Ranger said gently. "I ain't goin' to hurt yuh."

The eyes were staring, fear-crazed. Hatfield spoke soothingly, squatted there. After a time he reached in his hand, but the man shrank from him. It was horrible. The Ranger felt the deepest pity, for he knew what abuse the creature had received at the hands of the sadistic rustlers.

He brought some water and food from the cookshed, and offered it. This seemed to allay some of the prisoner's fear, and as Hatfield kept his voice gentle, trying to reach him, he came out into the light.

His face was overgrown with beard, matted, dirty, his hair sticking up from his head. The blue eyes had a terrible light in them, the anguish of one who has been tortured. Hatfield stared at him. In the better light, he saw the whitish, triangular-shaped scar on the left temple, and his heart seemed to jump into his throat.

"It — it couldn't be!" he croaked. He licked his lips, suddenly dry. "Cuss them!" he thought. "Cuss them!"

Icy fury at Carns and his terrible gang, and at what they had done swept him. He straightened up, and went over to the door. "Fenton!" he called.

The rancher chief, in charge at the house, was getting ready to receive the women and children they must protect, but came outside at the call.

"Come here," ordered the Ranger. "But brace yoreself."

He led Fenton to the chained man at the back of the building.

"Look at him," he growled.

John Fenton stared for moments. Suddenly he uttered a shrill cry and, stooping, seized the unfortunate in his arms.

"Nat! Nat! My boy!"

It was hard for the Ranger to maintain

his aplomb, as the father, wildly joyful for a time at having found his son, realized that Nat Fenton was no longer himself. He was alive, but the mind was not that of his son.

"Let's take him inside, Fenton," said the Ranger. "Help me tote him."

He had to find a chisel to break the chain, which had been stapled into the rock, and fastened to loops by a blacksmith, one of the outlaws who worked at a small forge where the rustlers could shoe their horses and work what metal they desired.

But this metal work had been done for the torture of a human being!

Chapter XIII

Carns' Ultimatum

Nat Fenton let his father handle him. He was docile, and some of the fear had left his blue eyes. He lay down on one of the bunks in a side room, when he was taken inside.

Fenton set about cleaning his son, changing his clothing, and trying to talk to him. Hatfield found a razor. He had Fenton soothe Nat, while he carefully cut the chestnut hair from the young fellow's head, to examine the head injury which had so affected Nat Fenton's mind.

"What do you think?" John Fenton's voice was strained, appealing, as he questioned the Ranger after the examination had been made.

Hatfield shrugged. "I can tell you a lot about gunshot and knife wounds, Fenton. A head injury's somethin' else. Looks to me like a piece of his skull's caved in there. It'd take a real good sawbones to give yuh the truth."

"We got to take him out, then, and find

such," declared Fenton.

It was over an hour before Sam Tate and Jack Fenton returned, wet to the waist, and scratched by rocks and thorns, to report that somehow the Indian squaw had eluded them.

"Must have hid herself somewheres along the river," said Sam. "We went downstream first, but we never did find any tracks of her. Reckon she waded in the water to hide 'em."

"Looks like there's a way out of the Pecos canyon somewheres upstream," said Jack. "That squaw hid on us, and mebbe she even got out of the ravine without us spottin' her."

Hatfield did not intend to remain long at the outlaw stronghold. He set his guards, awaiting the coming of the main party, with the women and children, and then found a quiet spot where he could snatch a little sleep.

Late in the afternoon, the canyon darkened as the sun declined, and the other settlers arrived, led by the guides who had been sent out for them. The bustle and stir awoke the Ranger. He was hungry and thirsty, and paid a visit to the well-stocked storehouse and cookshed.

When he got to the main house, Mrs.

Fenton and Em Tate, ushered by John Fenton, were entering the bedroom where Nat was lying. Obviously Fenton had not told them until now that Nat had been found alive. Hatfield could see them through the open doorway as they gathered about the young man, the hope of their lives.

"Son — son!"

The mother threw herself on her knees, to kiss Nat's face, cradling him in her arms as she had when he was a baby. But he did not respond, just stared. Emily, with tears flowing from her eyes, took his hand. As Nat looked at her a troubled expression came into his eyes.

"Nat, don't you know me?" she pleaded.

Hatfield turned away. The spectacle was heartrending. He went outside, and hunted up his saddle and bags, the gear which he had been forced to leave behind when he had escaped in the night. Goldy had been brought in by the main party of settlers and he saw to his horse.

He called John Fenton, as the darkness gathered over them.

"I'm goin' out and scout around, Fenton," he said. "I want to keep an eye on Pecos Carns. That squaw may reach him. So be on yore guard night and day. Watch both ends of the canyon trail, and re-member, the boys and I came down those rock ledges from above. Yuh got plenty of food and plenty of guns and ammunition, and yuh can hold out forever. I'll figger out the next move."

"Seems like a miracle, Ranger!" Fenton said gratefully. "It was a mighty smart play to come here. Thanks to you, we're safe and sound for a while."

John Fenton had hold of himself now. He had steeled his soul to the blows of Fate. Strength of character showed in the grim set of his lips. He did not say any-thing about Nat, the elder son he so loved, but he did not need to. Hatfield was able to read and understand his thoughts.

"Yeah, sooner or later Carns'll be back," drawled the Ranger. "As for Nat — he needs an expert's hands. The quicker the better, I reckon . . . Fenton, I want a few strong young fellers with me, who'll obey my orders — say Jack Junior, Sam, Barney Porter and two more. I've been turnin' somethin' over in my mind this afternoon. What do yuh say we carry Nat out, and send him by railroad to El Paso? There's good surgeons there, and a couple of the boys can go along with him on the train."

Fenton's eyes lighted. He seized Hatfield's hand, pressed it. . . .

Dark had fallen when the Ranger led his small band from the hide-out along the trail past the narrows. He had five young fighters at his heels, and Nat Fenton was secured on a strong black mustang, which Jack led.

They reached the upper trails without trouble, and headed through the rough country toward Fentonville. The railroad lay many hours' ride to the south. Hatfield was gambling that the young men and Nat could reach it before they were intercepted by the vicious enemies of the Pecos range.

Some little time before they were near Fentonville, Hatfield called the young men to give them their orders. Obediently Jack Fenton and another youth left the party, with Nat in tow, and changed direction to ride for the railroad, hoping to catch the morning train for El Paso.

As soon as they were out of sight, Jim Hatfield, Barney Porter, and one of Fred Whittemore's sons who had come with the Ranger, rode on toward Fentonville. They traveled cautiously and silently, but it was not a great while before their goal was in sight. Hatfield pulled up Goldy and sat his saddle, staring at the twinkling lights of Fentonville, below them in the valley.

"Come here, Barney," ordered the Ranger, and young Porter obediently pushed up beside his leader.

"Yes, suh," said Barney. His eyes gleamed in the silver sheen of the moon.

"I'm goin' into town and snoop around some," said Hatfield. "I want yuh to hold the boys here, but if yuh need to avoid trouble, go to it. I'll be back soon as I can. Don't do nothin' rash."

"We shore won't, Ranger." Young Porter's lithe shoulders squared as he drew in a deep breath and took responsibility proudly.

It was vital to watch the enemy's movements. Hatfield rode as near to the town as he dared, then dismounted and left Goldy, advancing on foot after he had traded his spurred riding boots for a pair of Indian moccasins. He always carried them as part of his equipment for scouting work. He also left his big Stetson with his boots, and rubbed dirt on his face, so that his skin would not shine in the dimness of night.

It was after midnight, but in Fentonville lamps were blazing in the saloon, in Barstowe's office, and in cabins. The savage rustlers had completely taken over the settlement. No doubt they held the few townsmen as hostages, allowing no one to leave.

The Ranger crept in, and lay behind a clump of brush, to reconnoiter. After a time a rider came slowly past him, a carbine slung on his shoulder and Colts in his holsters — a mounted sentinel, making the rounds. He connected with another further along before turning to come back on his post.

A warm wind picked up gritty sand to throw in Hatfield's face. The stars were magnificent in the vast dome of the sky, and the moon was dropping in the west. Hatfield watched the sentries, to learn their system. On the next tour of the horsemen, the Ranger crawled past the line and hid in a shallow split in the earth. Bit by bit, he worked closer to the shadowed rear of Barstowe's office.

There were enemies all around him, and guards patrolling the roads in all directions. Even as he reached his vantage point, he saw a guard pass the lighted window behind Barstowe's offices. There were sounds from the little saloon which was filled with drinkers who were rapidly drying up the oasis. Some were drunk, and their raucous cries rang in the night.

Hatfield waited for another twenty minutes, and noted that the sentry behind the office building came past the window point twice in that time. He would patrol the back, then turn up alongside the Central Pecos Development Company's quarters, no doubt to make a connection with another guard at the front. Pecos Carns was taking no chances.

Worming forward when the sentry's back was to him, Hatfield finally reached the carriage shed, not far from the main building. He could rest there, and watch his chance, and from this spot he saw Pecos Carns' tall figure restlessly pacing the office. There were several aides with the King of the Rustlers. But though the window was open to the warm night, he could not spy Silas Barstowe.

"Wonder if I could get up on that flat roof?" he mused, as the sentinel paced slowly past the rear window. "I could hear 'em from there."

At the right hand corner was a drain pipe, and the structure was a single-story one. But he needed to divert the guard's attention in order to reach the vantage point he desired. Suddenly, as he watched, the guard in sight came to life. He raised his carbine and ran toward the outside corner of the building. Hatfield tensed. For a moment he wondered if the sentry had glimpsed him, but then the wind brought the beat of mustang hoofs.

"Halt, there!" ordered the sentry as the hoof beats stopped. "Who're you!"

"Ees me — Conchita!" a woman's wailing voice answered.

"What's up?" called Pecos Carns, sticking his head and shoulders out the side window.

Everybody's attention was focused for the moment on the new arrival. Hatfield slid through the shadows, reached the inner corner, and his powerful arms drew him up the drain pipe. In a jiffy he was lying flat on the roof, edging toward that rear window.

"Hey, it's our squaw, Conchita!" sang out the sentinel.

"What's the matter, Conchita?" demanded Carns.

"Oh, senor — senor!" The squaw spoke broken English mixed with Spanish words and imprecations. "Bad hombres come! Zey tak' hacienda —"

The squaw was panting for breath. She was the one who had escaped from the hide-out in the creek canyon. Somehow she had caught a mustang and ridden the last miles to Fentonville. As Carns swore, she told of the capture of the outlaw stronghold by the Ranger and John Fenton's forces.

Pecos Carns began to whistle shrilly, calling his men. Rustlers left their carousing or woke from sleep, and came hurrying to answer him. All at once Fentonville seemed alive with tough, heavily armed killers, swarming to the offices.

"Cuss it!" Hatfield heard Carns saying. "This is that dirty Ranger's doin'! He's led 'em in there, boys."

"At leas'," said a Mexican's voice, "we hav' zose ranchos, Pecos."

"Yeah! And Barstowe's gone to El Paso! I can't leave here, not altogether. But we can't let Fenton and the Ranger keep our hide-out. It's goin' to be tough chasin' 'em out — but by hook or crook, I'll kill every one of 'em 'cept the women! They can stay and work for us."

Carns was ready to explode with his fury, and his profanity heated the air.

"What yuh mean to do, Pecos?" asked one of his cronies.

"We can't leave go of the town altogether, but we got to hustle over and take back our stronghold," Carns said. "I hate to do it, but we'll have to split our forces. I'll leave a holdin' force here, say twenty men under you, Kansas Joe. Me'n the rest'll head for home and get in by way of the river. They won't be lookin' for us that way, mebbe, and it's easier to rush than the pass in the crik canyon."

The Ranger lay quiet as Pecos Carns issued his commands. The King of the Rustlers went out into the main street. His fierce bearded followers then listened as he spoke to them.

"We're goin' to take back the place, boys — and we ain't sparin' any lives, savvy? Now get yore guns and plenty of ammunition, and saddle up. We're leavin' here in fifteen minutes!"

Chapter XIV

Fire!

During the excitement, the sentinels had rushed to the front. Hatfield snaked down the pipe, and stole back the way he had come. Picking up Goldy, he rode swiftly away, and found his three young allies watching for him.

"Sam," he said to Tate's son, "I got an important job for you. You ride like the devil was after yuh back to the folks. Tell 'em Carns is comin' with thirty men, to attack. They'll be there by dawn. They're goin' to make their main thrust by way of the Pecos. They savvy a way down near the mouth of the crik. Got it?"

"Yes, suh."

Sam Tate eagerly repeated the instructions. Then he rode off in the night, to take the warning to John Fenton.

Barney Porter and Hank Whittemore trailed the tall Ranger as Hatfield circled well around to the south of the settlement, and waited while Pecos Carns, with his hard-bitten crew, got started. They heard the many hoofs shaking the ground as the rustlers picked up speed, and could see the dark bulk of the band headed northwest for the stronghold.

The Ranger rested, and they took it easy for half an hour more, allowing Carns plenty of time to get out of earshot. The saloon and Barstowe's office remained lighted. Kansas Joe, in charge while Carns was gone, had a few sentries in the streets.

Hatfield had made his plans. He told them to the boys, and gave them instructions. They were delighted at the prospect of action.

Barney Porter and Hank moved to the north of Fentonville, while the Ranger started in again, afoot. As he had earlier, he began working his way to the south end of town where stood the offices of the CPD Company. He meant to get inside Barstowe's office this time, and when he left the contents of that informative file — the quit-claim deeds and notes assigning the great development — would go with him. He would rest easier, once they were destroyed, as he had told himself before.

Hidden in a small barn, he waited. Soon he heard Indian war-whoops, and violent shooting. Barney and his friend were raising the sky up at the far end of town, acting under his orders.

Carns' rustlers emerged, hastily running toward the hullabaloo. Most of them dashed in that direction, and Hatfield ran lightly to the back of Barstowe's office. He glanced in. The front door stood wide open, but the room was empty. Joe had run out into the road to see what was going on.

Hatfield thrust a long leg over the sill, and ducked inside. The big file containing the vital papers stood against the wall. Hastily he checked, to see if these had been removed. They were still in the drawers, as he had hoped. Barstowe, no doubt, had cautioned Carns to watch them closely while he hurried to set out for El Paso.

He was hastily tumbling the papers from the file onto the floor, meaning to scoop them up into a burlap bag, when he heard a wild yell from the front door.

"Hey, what the devil!"

Kansas Joe jumped into the office, leaping for Hatfield whose arms were full of papers. In his angry haste Joe did not watch where he was going, and lunged against the table set between him and the Ranger. It went over with a crash, and the jangle of broken glass as the oil lamp on the table went with it.

Instead of going out, though, the lamp wick was blazing high with more oil as the shattered fragments of the lamp fell squarely into the piled papers on the floor. They caught instantly, and yellow flames licked swiftly, hungrily on.

There was a wry grin on the Ranger's face as, with a sudden movement, he dropped the whole mass of papers in his arms into the licking flames. This suited him exactly. It would save him trouble. He had thought all the time those papers should be burned. It was real nice of Carns' lieutenant to attend to it so promptly.

"Fire!" shrieked Kansas Joe.

In that moment of panic the rustler saw the flames rising into the air, taking hold of all the papers that had been in the file. He had been ordered to guard those papers, and now they were ablaze. And standing coolly a few feet from the bonfire was Ranger Jim Hatfield, whom Kansas Joe had met, to his sorrow.

Hatfield's blue-steel Colts reposed in their holsters. His slim hands hung at his hips, relaxed. His feet were spread, and he slouched a little from the waist.

Kansas Joe felt an icy thrill up and down his spine, and the goose-flesh prickled his dirty hide. His black eyes snapped as he threw himself around, his glance riveted to that of the Ranger who watched him steadily.

"Cuss yuh — I got yuh this time!" howled the rustler.

His hand flew to the heavy revolver at his side. It cleared leather, rising to pin the Ranger. A shot blared in the room, then a second seemed joined to it. But it was Kansas Joe who staggered, tried to steady himself against the wall. A yard in front of the tall officer a jagged hole appeared in the mat, where Joe's slug had struck.

That outlaw Colt had never climbed high enough for Joe to kill his opponent. Before he could make it, a paralyzing sensation had stricken Kansas Joe. He fought it, his mouth wide, eyes rolling. The pistol clattered from his nerveless fingers. He clawed at his throat, turned, and fell across the door-sill, his head and shoulders slipping through until he lay partly outside.

Blue smoke drizzled from the Ranger Colt. Hatfield, eyes dark as an Arctic sea, waited a moment. Up the road, harsh shouts and gunshots told that Barney Porter and Hank Whittemore still were stirring up the enemy, giving Hatfield the opportunity to do his job.

It was getting hot in there. The Ranger

felt the heat from the mounting blaze on his right cheek, and moved off, backing toward the window. He was almost there when another rustler — one they called "Dinny" — appeared outside the open door, and bent curiously over Kansas Joe.

"What's the matter, Joe? Yuh drink too many?"

Then he saw the blood on the man's shirt and, glancing inside, saw the reddening light, the fire, and the tall figure at the window.

"Ranger!" he howled.

Dinny was quick, and his fear-stricken senses worked with lightninglike speed, as he sought to save himself. He threw himself flat, and Hatfield's bullet sang savagely over his head. Dinny rolled off, out of sight.

"Fire!" Hatfield heard him screaming. "Fire! The Ranger's here! Pronto, boys — help-p!"

Hatfield ducked from the window, and ran lightly to the alleyway, so that he could watch the section of main road along which the outlaws would come, in answer to Dinny's frantic cries. Guns loaded, he waited. Soon several rustlers padded up, and Hatfield opened up on them with his revolvers. They jumped back, for cover.

The fire had licked up the wooden wall. The big wooden file was a mass of flames, roaring furiously, and the papers had all been consumed. The hot breath of the fire would prevent men from approaching that file closely now, to try to save what they believed was in it. They would need a bucket line to put that fire out now. The office ceiling was smoking as the Ranger ran back to the carriage shed. He knew his foes would try to circle the other buildings as quickly as possible.

Soon stealthy figures showed against the red light. A tongue of flame licked out a side window. The wind brought the hot smell of the conflagration. Hatfield fired on a couple of rustlers and they answered, the stabbing explosions staining the air.

The outer wall of the office building began to smoke. The dry wood took hold, and the windows the Ranger could see were ruby red. Evidently the office was a seething mass of flames.

As he waited, holding the gang's attention with his guns, several loud pops came from the structure like giant corn smashing its shell. Then hundreds of little whooshes ensued.

"Sounds like ammunition goin' off!" thought Hatfield. "By gravy they must

156

have looted it from the store and brought it here to the office to guard it!"

The building was beyond saving. Certainly the file and the papers were consumed. Barstowe would have only force to depend upon when he tried to seize the ranches of John Fenton and the other settlers.

Satisfied with the night's work here, the Ranger turned and ran. Shrill whistles came from his lips, and soon the golden sorrel galloped to him. He mounted and rode away from the settlement and the rustler guns.

The two youths had drawn off as the rustlers had sought to engage them. Then the fire and the frantic shouts of the other outlaws had forced the pursuers to turn and hurry back into town. When the lads recognized Hatfield they came riding to him. The trio sat their saddles for a time, watching the mounting blaze and the futile attempts of the enemy to control it.

"That was a mighty good thing to happen for all of us, Ranger," Barney Porter said soberly. "What now?"

"This'll hold 'em for a while," drawled Hatfield. "And I reckon the folks can hold that crik canyon fort for a few days. How'd you fellers like to take a run to El Paso?"

"Huh?" gloated Barney, and Hank echoed his sentiments.

El Paso had recently become accessible to other portions of the huge state of Texas when a railroad had been built with the town as a terminal and it was a mecca for anyone who loved excitement. It was growing rapidly, and it drew undesirable as well as decent citizens. Its reputation as a spot where anything might happen was enhanced by lurid tales. Such a town naturally fascinated the youngsters, and the prospect of a visit to it thrilled them.

"I'm takin' you boys along," said Hatfield. "I got business there — Barstowe's gone to El Paso. We'll head for the railroad and flag the first train west. . . ."

It was noon when the creaking train ground to a jarring stop at the El Paso station, and Jim Hatfield, with his eager charges, jumped from the high step of the car to the wooden platform.

The town, growing with mushroom rapidity, was regularly laid out on bottom lands, stretching to the slopes northeast and northwest of the settlement. It was a port of entry and county seat of El Paso county.

Across the Rio Grande lay Mexico, the town opposite El Paso being Paso del Norte. A large trade went on between the two countries, and smugglers as well as merchants made the city a headquarters. Lead mines outside the city, and vast salt lakes, and saloons that catered to a tremendous, unquenchable thirst for alcoholic liquors and other entertaining vices on the part of a large proportion of its citizenry were the chief sources of industry and revenue. Gamblers plied their trade in the saloons and gunmen and gunfighters, strutting and preening themselves, and having it out, kept the inhabitants from perishing of ennui.

Hatfield believed that his work in El Paso might prove dangerous, and he did not wish to expose Barney Porter and young Whittemore to a daylight gun battle in which one or both might be cut down. He would move against Silas Barstowe alone.

They found an eating place near the station, and when they had finished their meal Hatfield paid the bill. He furnished the youths with spending money with which to amuse themselves, and then set about locating Silas Barstowe's office in the town, walking because he had left Goldy and the boys' mounts with the stationmaster at the little tank stop on the railroad, back where they had caught the train.

Colorful vaqueros in handsome steeple-peak sombreros and velvet clothing, peons in dirty white and straw hats, their bare feet splayed in the dirt of the road, passed him. There were ladies out shopping, and brown, white and red children played in the streets.

The sun gleamed on the whitewashed haciendas standing in their grounds on the hills around the town. It beat impartially on the hovels of the Mexican quarter below in the sand. Gamblers, outlaws on vacation or watching for a prospect, and their women friends were indoors for the most part. They disliked the brightness of the day.

A large saloon, the batwings invitingly hooked open, drew the Ranger. He glanced around to make sure the lads were not following him, and went inside. A white-aproned bartender came to serve him. The bar was ornate, with long crystal mirrors gleaming behind it. Hatfield ordered whisky, and the barkeeper chatted with him as he drank.

"Yuh acquainted with Silas Barstowe?" Hatfield inquired, after he had made friendly contact.

"Barstowe?" the barber repeated. "Yuh mean the land broker? Don't know him, exactly, but I know he's got an office up the street. Two blocks — biggest buildin' in the town."

Chapter XV

Hot Town

Vital and commanding as he strode down the sidewalk toward the new office building towering before him, Jim Hatfield's tall, rugged figure drew the eyes of all passersby. Instinctively women noticed the mighty Ranger — but so did men.

In front of an office on the far side of the street a freshly painted sign proclaimed in bold letters:

SILAS BARSTOWE — INVESTMENTS

Hatfield looked around for sentries, for he believed that Barstowe might be on the alert, watching in case he should have been trailed from Fentonville. But so far as he could see, the place was unguarded. The Ranger walked across the street and glanced through an open window. Several customers sat inside, and barring the way to an inner sanctum was a girl employee in a dark skirt and white shirtwaist.

Ready for anything, Hatfield entered. The customers glanced up at him but nobody seemed excited. Seeing a closed door behind the girl's desk which said "Dr. Barstowe" in gilt print the Ranger moved over to the girl.

"Dr. Barstowe in, ma'am?" he asked.

"No, sir. He's out eating. But he'll be back."

She was a comely girl with a wealth of dark hair prettily arranged on her well-shaped head. Her long lashes fluttered as she met the rugged officer's gray-green gaze. Apparently his looks appealed to her.

"I'll wait, if it's all right," he said. "I'm interested in Fentonville."

"It's very popular," she murmured.

"Any property left?" he inquired.

"A few choice places, I think. But a good many people have started there, to take up holdings."

"I see."

He sat down at the end of a bench, and his glance roved over the framed mottoes on the walls. "Handsome Is As Handsome Does!" "Honesty Is The Best Policy," "A Rolling Stone Gathers No Moss."

"Barstowe loves 'em," he mused.

A map of Fentonville and its environs was on one wall. A decidedly imaginative artist had painted it, for it was depicted as a thriving metropolis in the center of numerous big ranches. Here and there ornate pictures showed the advantages: "Concrete Dam" — and in small letters, "To be completed." "Plaza & Fountain — will be built." "Main Railroad Station — Construction assured." A courthouse, schoolhouse and other inducements were "promised," or "assured" or "contemplated."

The office furnishings were glittering and new. A first-class bucketshop operator never let his front grow dingy.

This time Barstowe had what he considered a watertight proposition. The land and buildings he was selling actually existed and he held legal claims on these tangible assets. Anything exaggerated in the advertising was covered by modifying phrases.

"Cuss him, he's livin' like a prince and runnin' his business like a decent person, while those folks at Fentonville suffer!"

A handsome equipage drawn by two shining livery stable horses drew up at the curb. The driver jumped down and opened the door, and Silas Barstowe emerged. He wore dark trousers, a frock coat and a new top-hat. A cane was snugged under one arm, and a diamond glittered in his cravat.

His sideburns had been freshly trimmed, and he was smoking a long black cheroot.

At sight of him there was a quickening among the eager customers in the room. But Barstowe did not come in the front way. He turned to a side entry where there was a private door to his office. Hatfield saw four men, with Colts strapped about their waists, taking up positions.

"Bodyguard," he decided. They no doubt had been eating and drinking while Barstowe was having his meal.

The Ranger glided toward the sanctum door. A well-dressed man of around fifty reached the secretary's desk before him and as Hatfield started past, the customer said:

"I'm first, young feller!"

"Yes, sir, this gentleman's ahead of you," said the girl. "You'll have to wait. Dr. Barstowe's very busy but he'll see you as soon as —"

"He'll see me now," said Hatfield gently, but firmly.

Her red lips parted. She was frightened, and suddenly she screamed:

"Oh — I know who you are! It's you!"

"Keep quiet," warned the Ranger.

He tried the door but it was bolted. He put a shoulder to it, and the bolts' screws tore out of the wood.

The secretary's cry had been heard inside. Silas Barstowe stood at the rear of his sanctum. His pink face went a shade redder as he recognized Hatfield.

The inner office was elegantly furnished, with a red carpet and a mahogany desk and easy chairs. New mottoes and a map of Fentonville were on the walls and vases of flowers, boxes of cigars, decanters and crystal glasses on the desk.

"Stop him!" shrieked Barstowe.

The benevolence had left his face. His big nose twitched like a rabbit's. He was mortally afraid.

"Yuh're under arrest, Barstowe," snapped the Ranger.

He broke off. Two of the bodyguards in black trousers, dark string ties, white shirts, and narrow-brimmed Stetsons had leaped forward.

"Stand aside, boys," warned the Ranger. "I'm a Texas Ranger — Hatfield's the name."

With a squeak of fear, Barstowe threw himself down and through the door into a rear room. The side door opened and a couple more sentries pushed through. Hatfield was moving swiftly when a gun roared from the left. But the bullet missed, and he made his own draw, forced to fight.

Women screamed in the outer office, and everybody not involved hunted cover. The fellow who had fired shrieked as Ranger lead cut into his gun arm. He fell to one knee, bent over, gripping his wound.

"Out of the way, or I'll blow yuh out!" ordered Hatfield.

The guards who had been blocking the way, shocked by the determined speed of the officer made no further attempt to check him. They pushed back and let him run by, on the broker's trail, Colt in hand.

The rooms in the rear of the private office were furnished with bunks and some chairs. It looked as though the sentries, Barstowe's guard, might live here. An open door led into the alley, and through it the broker had fled. When Hatfield reached the narrow way, Barstowe was not in sight.

"Cuss it, he was all ready for me," he thought.

He began hunting up and down for his quarry, aware that one of Barstowe's men was watching him through a window at the rear of the offices. The back door of a big saloon and gambling parlor came into sight.

Piles of rusting tin cans, over which hovered swarms of insects, almost blocked his path. He could look through the corridor into the bar, and see the light over and under the batwings at the street.

Hatfield turned into the saloon. A few customers were inside, and the white-aproned bartenders stared at him as he approached.

"See an hombre with side whiskers, in a frock coat, come through, boys?" the Ranger asked.

One of them nodded, pointed to the batwings.

"Went out thataway. Yuh mean Doc Barstowe?"

"That's him."

The elusive Barstowe could move fast when he needed to. He was not on the street when the Ranger emerged from the saloon. Hatfield had to take a chance on which direction the fugitive had chosen. The offices lay to Hatfield's right, but he turned left. The gunshots had been heard, and a crowd was collecting to watch Barstowe's place, although the curious kept at a safe distance.

There was another big saloon a few doors down, the Oxford. Hatfield turned into it, to see if anyone there had noticed the fleeing Barstowe.

The barkeep shook his head at the

Ranger's question, and shrugged.

"Didn't see him, mister."

Hatfield pinned on his Ranger star, as he left the Oxford, and crossed the street. There were many large places of amusement in the city and he chose one at random, the Oasis. But no one had seen Barstowe.

As he pushed the batwings to emerge from the Oasis a hoarse voice shouted:

"Reach!"

He had to make his decision instantly. For a round-headed, blunt-bodied man in brown clothing and straight Stetson stood within a dozen feet, with a sawed-off shotgun in his hands leveled at the Ranger.

Hatfield might have jumped back into the saloon, his Colts roaring, had he not seen the badge on the man's vest. It was a city marshal's official star, and the Rangers played along with such local lights of the law when they were honest. To fight now might mean the death of innocent bystanders.

"All right, Marshal," he called. "I'm a Texas Ranger, chasin' a fugitive. His handle's Silas Barstowe."

"Uh-huh!"

The black eyes of the big shotgun barrels were now firmly pinned on the Ranger, and the deputies with the city marshal had their weapons up. Someone would get hurt, if the big man moved for his Colts. Besides, Hatfield was sure that this marshal was a bonafide officer, and such an official would assist the State Rangers.

"I want Barstowe for killin' and attempted killin', as well as other things, Marshal," he said. "S'pose yuh give me a hand?"

The determined set of the marshal's jaw did not change.

"Go up behind him and take his shootin' irons, Harry," he said to one of his deputies.

"Wait! I ain't givin' up my guns, Marshal. Let's palaver."

Something was wrong here. Was this another of Barstowe's tricks, and this man merely posing as a marshal? If so, then why hadn't he cut down the Ranger?

"We'll palaver at the jail, feller," the marshal growled. "Yuh'll do as I say. I'm Jack Greggs, marshal of this town."

"I've heard tell of yuh, Greggs. They say yuh're a good man."

The marshal frowned. "Start movin' — keep yore hands up."

Hatfield could choose between almost certain death, for Greggs or himself, and obedience. With a shrug of his wide shoulders, he raised his hands and walked up the sidewalk, the marshal at his heels, his deputies alert.

The courthouse jail, to which Hatfield had intended to escort Silas Barstowe, stood two blocks down the street. As they moved toward it Greggs was wary.

He did not insist that the prisoner shed his guns until they reached the steps of the lockup.

Then he ordered Hatfield to unbuckle his belts and let them drop, his back to the officers.

Barstowe was gone by now. It was necessary to clear up the situation, and Hatfield resigned himself to the delay.

Jack Greggs, never relaxing his vigilance, forced him to the cell-block, and not until the lock had clicked on the Ranger did the marshal heave a sigh of relief, and his face broke its severe lines.

"That'll hold yuh for a while, till the judge comes back," he said.

Hatfield took hold of the door bars, staring out at the marshal.

"Yuh're makin' a bad mistake, Greggs. I didn't put up a fight for I savvy yuh're an honest hombre. But what's the idea? Yuh've arrested and locked up a state officer. I'm Ranger Jim Hatfield and I'm on an important job. Figgered yuh'd help me, instead of fightin' me."

This did not have any effect on Greggs. He smiled, a little sardonically.

"It's no use. I savvy just who yuh are. That yarn won't help yuh none, Miles."

A cold shock swept Hatfield. "Yuh figger I'm Acey Miles?"

"Exactly."

Hatfield scratched his head. A wry grin touched his wide mouth.

"I reckon Barstowe's tricked yuh somehow, Greggs. Yuh better start checkin'. Who told yuh I'm Acey Miles? Barstowe?"

"Barstowe? Yuh mean Si Barstowe? He's a respected citizen here, feller. No doubt yuh tried to get some money out of him."

Jack Greggs was a brave man, thought the Ranger, but he was not too bright. The marshal was proud of his capture of the supposed badman.

He turned a deaf ear to Hatfield's arguments, and left the cell-block.

Chapter XVI

Explosive

Early dusk was almost at hand, for it was getting late in the afternoon. Through the little barred window at the end of the block, the sun streamed, as it dropped westward. A drunken man in the other wing was singing snatches of a ribald song. Hatfield sat down, rolled a smoke, and made himself as comfortable as he could.

"Wonder if that judge has quit for the day?" he mused. If so, it meant spending the night in jail.

Another hour passed, before he heard Greggs' footsteps. The marshal had come for him.

"Judge is settin', Miles. Come on. Behave yoreself, now!"

He was wary as he prodded the prisoner through a dark corridor into the courtroom, guarded by armed men. The judge sat at his bench. He inspected the captive over his eyeglasses.

"What's the charge, Marshal?" he asked.

"This hombre is one Acey Miles, a well-known outlaw, Judge. He's wanted for killin's in half a dozen counties. There's two thousand dollars reward for him and I guess I win." Greggs preened himself.

"What have yuh to say before I bind yuh over?" the judge asked Hatfield.

"Judge, the marshal's makin' a mistake," said the Ranger softly. "I'm Jim Hatfield, Texas Ranger."

"Huh?" The magistrate frowned. "What about this, Marshal?"

"That's his way of playin' his game, Judge. Look at this!"

Triumphantly, Jack Greggs took a telegram from his pocket and laid it before the judge, who scanned it.

"Can I see that, suh?" asked Hatfield.

Without comment, the magistrate passed it to Hatfield, who read:

ACEY MILES WANTED FOR KILLINGS IN GOLIAD FAYETTE AND CALDWELL COUNTIES REWARDS AMOUNTING TWO THOUSAND DOLLARS HEADED FOR EL PASO STOP DANGEROUS WILL SHOOT TO KILL IF CORNERED STOP SIX FOOT THREE BROAD SHOULDERS

BLACK HAIR AND POSES AS TEXAS RANGER NAMED JIM HATFIELD HOLD FOR SHERIFFS OF ABOVE COUNTIES STOP TOM VALE MARSHAL ALPINE TEXAS.

Hatfield thought rapidly. Alpine was a stop on the railroad between El Paso and the tank station which was nearest Fentonville.

"Now I savvy, Judge," he said. "The hombre I'm after, a slick operator named Barstowe, sent this message from Alpine on his way here from Fentonville."

The judge scowled severely at Greggs, who was blinking, losing a little of his assurance.

"Yuh shore yuh ain't made a bad mistake, Greggs?" demanded the judge. "This man don't look like a criminal to me and I've seen plenty in my time. Who said he was Miles? How'd yuh come to arrest him?"

"Come to think of it," admitted Greggs, his composure rapidly cracking, "it was one of the fellers from Barstowe's office who run up and told me Miles was loose!"

"Why not wire Cap'n McDowell at

Austin and settle it?" suggested the Ranger.

"Go to it," ordered the judge.

It was dark before McDowell's sulphurous reply burned over the wires from Austin. Jack Greggs came in with it. His round face was crimson and he began apologizing profusely as he saw the Ranger.

The judge had waited around to see the outcome. Now he began to give the city marshal a severe tongue lashing, but Hatfield interfered.

"It's all right, Judge. I don't blame Greggs so much. Barstowe's a mighty slick hombre."

"Let me buy drinks, at least," begged Greggs. "I been a jackass, Ranger."

Lights blazed in the streets, and the town had picked up speed. Big saloons catered to the customers flocking to the bars. Workers, paid for the week, were hurrying to lose their earnings at the gambling tables, and gaudily dressed women were starting their evening. El Paso was beginning to roar.

Greggs bought drinks and barbecue at the Oxford. Then he went with Hatfield as the Ranger checked Barstowe's offices. They were dark, deserted.

"Yuh savvying where the cuss lives, Greggs?"

"I think he hangs out at the Metropolitan Hotel."

They knew Greggs at the hotel, and let him into the two rooms which had been Barstowe's living quarters.

"He's packed up and run for it," said Hatfield, as they looked over the place.

Articles of clothing were scattered about. Barstowe had hastily packed a bag, and departed. Searching through the two rooms, the Ranger picked up a telegram that had been sent to Barstowe from the tank town below Fentonville. It read:

NEED BLASTING POWDER TO COMPLETE PROJECT STOP URGENT STOP CARNS.

Greggs peered at it over the Ranger's shoulder.

"Blastin' powder!" he said. "What's that mean?"

"It means tall trouble for some folks I been tryin' to protect from Barstowe and Pecos Carns, King of the Rustlers. Let's see when this come in. I wonder if Barstowe had time to pick up that explosive?"

The time received on the wire was 3:32 PM, and Barstowe might well have taken a few minutes to get what Carns wanted.

176

"I'll check at the station, Greggs," Hatfield said. "He may have headed back to Fentonville to help out his pardner Carns. And then, I understand a good many customers have gone there and that means money in their pockets. Where's the city hospital?"

"Two blocks up and one over, big white buildin'."

"Will you and yore boys hunt through town for Barstowe, just in case, Greggs?"

"Shore, Ranger."

Hatfield hurried to the station. The agent had not sold Barstowe a ticket, but suggested that the fugitive might well have simply paid his fare on the train, which had pulled out at 4:30, headed east. By that time it had passed Alpine and there was no one but the agent at the tank stop below Fentonville. The next train was at five in the morning.

Greggs' unfortunate error had given Barstowe the time he needed to escape.

"I'll have to hustle back and try to stop their play," the Ranger thought. "They could blow that hide-out in the crik canyon to smithereens with grenades."

He went to hunt the boys who had made the trip with him, and whom he had turned loose shortly after noon. He found them at a restaurant, eating supper. When they were finished, they walked to the hospital, to inquire about Nat Fenton. They found Jack in an anteroom. He was astonished to see them in town.

"They're operatin' on Nat now," Jack informed the Ranger. "The doc ain't shore how it'll come out. He had to rest Nat up and get him ready, before he could go to work on him."

It was an hour before Hatfield could see the surgeon, a grave, bearded man.

"I've just finished," reported the doctor. "There was a depression in the skull exerting pressure on the boy's brain. It had to be lifted or he'd have remained out of his mind and perhaps eventually died from it. He was in bad shape generally, too. Evidently he had been beaten and starved. But he has a naturally strong constitution."

"He may pull through, then?"

"I'll know for sure in another twenty-four hours."

There was nothing to be done, except to wait for the morning train, wait until they knew whether Nat Fenton would live or die.

"I'm goin' to leave you and yore pard here, Jack," said the Ranger. "The rest of us'll go on back to Fentonville. You see to yore brother, and wire me at the tank stop how Nat comes along, savvy?"

When Hatfield and his two young comrades, Barney Porter and Hank Whittemore, reached the outskirts of Fentonville the town was filled with people. The three travelers sat their horses, watching the settlement.

They had checked up with the agent at the railroad stop which lay below. Barstowe had come to Fentonville the night before, when the express had paused to let him off. A couple of Carns' rustlers had been waiting for him.

There had been an influx of people, too, and men from Fentonville — no doubt Carns' followers — had been meeting the trains with wagons purloined from the town and ranches, and with saddles horses, to transport the customers to the development. There had been three prospective purchasers on the same train with Hatfield and the boys.

But evidently Carns and Barstowe felt they had enough fodder. They needed every man they could muster for the destruction of Fenton and his friends. They were in a hurry for they must collect the money from their victims, and escape before the Ranger could bring forces to overwhelm them.

"They must be mighty short of ammunition," the Ranger told the youths with him. "A lot went off in that fire, and they ain't been able to reach their stronghold. Can't have more'n a beltful or two per man."

Through his field-glass, he studied the town. Barstowe had his headquarters at his home for his office now was a black heap of ruin. The quit-claim deeds, the fancy stock certificates had been burned, but that would hardly check Barstowe. He could give forged deeds, anything to get his hands on the cash offered for the ranches by eager buyers inflamed by the rush at the development.

Flat wagons, buggies and saddle horses were returning to Fentonville, the vehicles driven by rustlers, containing customers.

"Been out to see their ranches, I reckon," mused the Ranger.

As they came in, the people stood in line outside Barstowe's to complete the deals.

Pecos Carns, the red-headed rustler chief, was there.

"Glad to see him," thought Hatfield. "I reckon he's huggin' close to Barstowe so's to get his share of the profits."

The outlaw had disposed of the few inhabitants of the town — the storekeeper, the bartender and the rest. No doubt the honest citizens were being held under guard in one of the buildings so that they could not disturb the business being transacted.

The sun was reddening as it lowered over the Trans-Pecos mountains. From the mesquite-screened height where Hatfield was hidden, he watched the enemy forces. He saw Pecos Carns go into Barstowe's shack and after a time he came out, carrying a square wooden box. Many of the buyers had completed the deals, and were hunting food and drink, and a place to spend the night in the little settlement.

"Must be the blastin' powder Carns has got!" Hatfield said grimly. "That's what has me worried. Come on, boys! We got to stop it."

Pecos Carns saddled up and tied the box to his saddle cantle. Accompanied by four of his men, he rode northwest from Fentonville.

"Not much light left, boys," said the Ranger. "It's up to us to catch Carns. Foller me but make it quiet when we get close to 'em."

They had worked north of the town, and now, keeping on the screened heights, they rode to cut off Pecos Carns when he swung toward his erstwhile stronghold.

Chapter XVII

Duel

Unseen by any of the men they were pursuing, since they were hidden by a ridge, Jim Hatfield and his two lithe trailmates galloped swiftly to head off Pecos Carns and his followers.

"Let's get into them rocks ahead, Ranger, and open up on 'em," said Barney Porter excitedly.

Hatfield shook his head. "The Rangers always give a man a chance to surrender, boys, no matter how bad he may be."

"It's takin' an awful risk, just the same," declared Barney. But he was impressed, and Hatfield could see that Barney Porter had filed this in his new code of behavior.

"You boys keep yore heads down and watch me for the cue, savvy? I don't want either of yuh hurt. Let's dismount. They'll be passin' this point in a short time."

They had come to the jagged boulders which commanded a turn of the beaten trail. There was not much light left, only a slice of the red sun showing over the peak. Hatfield unshipped his carbine. His manner was cool, there was no excitement in his attitude, and the lads watched him, imitating him. They had rifles loaded and ready as the three crouched in ambush by the trail.

Pecos Carns appeared at the bluff, and made the turn. He was closely followed by two of his rustlers, while the rest came in a bunch a few yards to the rear.

The King of the Rustlers was a magnificent rider. His fierce face was set, his emerald eyes fixed on the trail ahead.

Hatfield had a cartridge in the breech of his carbine, and his voice was sharp and steady as he called:

"Throw down, Carns! Yuh're covered!"

That sent the rustlers into spasms of shocked alarm. They rose inches from their saddles, and the mustangs, frightened at the sudden loud shout near at hand, fought their bits.

But Pecos Carns was not surrendering so easily. He ripped at his reins and one bony hand flew to the Colt at his bunched hip. The heavy stallion he was riding reared high on his hind legs, impelled by the violent jerk at his bit; its nostrils flared. And as Carns saw the Ranger's carbine leveled at his chest, he slid off the stallion, meaning to use the mount as a shield. But the frightened mustang fled, as Hatfield's gun roared. Barney Porter fired, past Hatfield, and a rustler who had hastily sought to get his Colt going threw up both hands, his gun flying to the ground. The man crashed dead on the trail.

Hatfield let go a second time. Another outlaw hastily ducked and, having swung his mustang, spurred back in retreat. The bunch at the rear, seeing Carns afoot and his stallion running away, were blocked for a moment and hesitated.

Hank Whittemore aimed at them, and fired. They felt the wind of the passing bullet, and then Hatfield jumped into the trail, facing Pecos Carns.

Carns was half-crouched. He had his Colt in his hand as he whirled around on Hatfield, who had thrown down his carbine. Violent profanity streamed from the mouth of the King of the Rustlers.

"Yuh'll never take me, cuss yore hide, Ranger!"

Pecos Carns loomed in the narrow path, gun in hand. The man was afraid, for he had seen the terrific fighting power of Jim Hatfield. There was a tremor to his hand as he threw up his gun. Hatfield was cool, even. His unhurried brain, his straight eyes, spelled death for his opponent.

Barney Porter, and Hank Whittemore, thrilled at the sight of their tall friend in action, held their breath. The little knot of rustlers, not daring to shoot because their leader was directly in front of them, stared open-mouthed at the scene. It occupied only fractions of time but it seemed much longer to the spectators.

Carns' revolver banged, and the Ranger Colt roared. Something kicked up the shale close to Jim Hatfield's left foot — Pecos Carns' slug.

With horrified eyes the stricken rustlers saw that their mighty chief, whom they had believed invulnerable, was losing all ability to control his limbs. They saw his gun arm drop, the pistol clatter to the path. His knees began to shake as though suddenly turned to rubber. The emerald eyes were wide, as was the gasping, fishy mouth seeking air that would not come into the paralyzed lungs. A bluish hole showed, where Hatfield's slug had smashed into Carns' nose. Blood spurted, and Pecos Carns went down, a miserable heap of carrion in the trail.

There was a tense silence. Then Barney Porter, with a hoarse cheer, fired again, and Hank Whittemore followed suit. The remaining rustlers, their chief down, turned tail and, splitting up, galloped away at top speed, low over their mustangs and thinking only of escape.

The two young fellows watched the tall Ranger check Pecos Carns, making sure that the King of the Rustlers had, as McDowell had drily put it, "been crowned." They saw the icy glint in the tall officer's eyes, the grim set of the rugged jaw.

That was how the Rangers fought. No matter what the odds they gave the worst of outlaws a chance to surrender before they opened fire. They accepted this disadvantage and beat their foes to the punch.

"Me — I'm goin' to be a Texas Ranger, if they'll have me, when I'm old enough," declared Barney Porter.

"Me, too," seconded Hank Whittemore.

"Thanks, boys," said Hatfield. "That's mighty flatterin'. I reckon yuh'll make fine Rangers."

There was work to be done. In the creek canyon hideout, John Fenton and his friends, including women and children, were in danger. Tough outlaws sought to kill them, and Hatfield knew that he must smash the rustlers.

He searched Carns and in one of the

rustler chief's saddle-bags he found a large amount of money.

"I'll take care of this, boys," he said. "It belongs to them folks that Barstowe sold yore people's ranches to. Si Barstowe has a lot more of it, and I aim to get as much as I can and return it to the rightful owners . . . Barney, reckon you and Hank can catch that mustang out there?"

The saddled horse which had belonged to Pecos Carns had run after the fleeing bunch for a time but, riderless, had slowed and put down his head to graze.

The light was almost gone as Barney and Hank hurried to do the Ranger's bidding. They returned to their horses and rode across the flats, lariats ready. A quick run, the skillful cast of the rope, and they came back on the trail, leading the spare mount.

Hatfield hoisted the remains of Pecos Carns to the back of his horse, and secured it with a rope. He took charge of the small box that was filled with explosives, which Carns had been taking in to the canyon to blow out the settlers who had invaded his stronghold.

Led by Hatfield, the small cavalcade hurried northwest. From the heights they could look back in the darkness and see the lights of Fentonville.

"Barstowe'll have to wait till we take care of them folks down there in the ravine," mused the Ranger.

Barney Porter yawned. He was sleepy, tired from the hard riding and excitement of the past days. So was Hank.

"We'll go into camp in the chaparral and spend the night, boys," said the Ranger. "We got to get an early start in the mornin'. Plenty to be done yet to make this range safe."

They were not many miles from the blind in-trails to the hide-out. Riding in the darkness might mean death at any moment for one of his young charges or himself. There might be rustlers at any bend, and there was nothing which Hatfield could do further until he had some light to work by.

He led the boys into the woods, and they unsaddled and made a fireless camp. They ate snacks from their saddle-bags, washing the cold food down with water from canteens. Then the two boys rolled in blankets, and were quickly asleep.

Hatfield left the body of Pecos Carns in the chaparral, and was soon asleep himself. . . .

He woke in the first gray touch of the new dawn. Barney and Hank slept on. The

Ranger got up, quietly checked their position, and saddled the horses. Then he woke the two lads, and they had more cold food for breakfast.

The creek canyon lay above them, northward. They were well away from the trail in, but the Ranger's marvelous sense of direction took them to the path which he had cut before, when he had first descended the shelves of rock into the canyon to help capture it when Fenton had attacked. They had to leave their horses, unsaddling the animals and allowing them freedom to roam.

Faint gray light covered the world. The sun was not yet showing when Hatfield peeked over the first drop, down into the canyon. A mist rose from the water far below, helping screen him and the two boys.

A gunshot came, faintly, from the direction of the Pecos down in the canyon. Two more cracked in reply. Hatfield could hear distant shouts, then a volley of rifles speaking from his left, toward the buildings and the narrow pass leading to them.

"Sounds like a dawn attack," he mused. "I better hustle."

He lowered Pecos Carns' body, and went down on the ropes himself, carrying the box of explosive powder with him. Barney and Hank quickly followed.

In the growing light, they descended from shelf to shelf, and the shooting rose in volume, mingled with hoarse shouts of fighting men.

"Seems like they're rushin' from both sides," he remarked to the boys.

They were almost to the final jump when a sharp challenge came from beneath them.

"Halt, there!"

They could see the muzzle of a rifle pointing their way, and the top of a Stetson. Barney Porter gave a cry of delight.

"Hey, Pop! Don't shoot! It's us!"

Chapter XVIII

"Throw Down, Rustlers"

Grim Ed Porter was the sentry on guard at the center. Fenton had not forgotten Hatfield's word of caution about the shelves of rock which made it possible for a man to descend. But the rustlers either had not thought of the route or hadn't considered it feasible.

"Barney, my boy!" Porter bobbed up, his bearded face glowing with joy. "I'm mighty glad to see yuh. Yuh ain't hurt, are yuh, son?"

"Nope, I'm fine. Had a fine time, too. I'm goin' to join the Rangers next year when I'm old enough, Pop."

"You come down here, right now," ordered Porter, "and look out for flyin' lead. They're hittin' us from both sides."

Hatfield jumped to the trail, after lowering Pecos Carns and the box to Porter. Hank and Barney joined him. Volleys came from either end of the canyon, and up the line Fenton and his contingent held the pass, while toward the river Fred Whittemore and another bunch of the settlers fought back the furious rustlers.

The women and children were safe inside the house, protected from stray bullets.

"So yuh held out all right," said the Ranger to Porter.

"Yeah, but we had a couple close shaves at night. They're awful mad, Ranger, and determined to finish us off and take back their hide-out. Couple of us got hit but we winged several of 'em when they tried to rush the pass."

"I reckon it's up to us to discourage 'em, then," Hatfield said. "Wait'll I find some empty tin cans."

There were piles of cans near the cook-shed, and the Ranger set about making crude grenades with the blasting powder, some horseshoe nails from the shop, lengths of fuse which he had found in the box, and the containers.

Soon he was ready. The sun had reddened the sky though shadows and dampness still prevailed down in the canyon.

A rancher came along the creek trail from the Pecos, limping, and with blood dripping from a wound in his leg.

"It's gettin' hot down there," he said to

Porter. "They've fetched in more men and we ain't got such good cover as at the pass."

The wounded settler went toward the house, where the women would care for his injury.

Hatfield fashioned half a dozen of the grenades, making the fuses short. Picking out and roping a rustler mustang which was in the little grazing park, he secured Pecos Carns to its back. Now he was ready.

He led the mustang down the rough path toward the river. Fred Whittemore, in command of twenty ranchers holding that side, recognized him, sang out to him.

"Ranger! Yuh're back. Keep down — they're shootin' from them high points to right and left!"

Hatfield took in the situation. The outlaws were dismounted, since they had come in by way of the Pecos canyon and had left their horses far above. They had carbines, and had worked into the rocks at either side. But they were careful with their fire, trying to make each bullet count.

"They're short of ammunition," he remembered.

Whittemore and the ranchers with him were keeping down, hugging the dirt. A sniper's slug shrieked past Hatfield's head.

Pecos Carns' remains, fastened to the mustang, bobbed up and down as the Ranger set the animal in motion down the creek bed.

"Make way for the King of the Rustlers!" roared the Ranger, his voice echoing in the deep, narrow canyon.

They heard him, and for a moment the gunfire slackened. The outlaws looked on their dead chief, and cold struck at their hearts. Hatfield, running forward, crouched at the side of a great boulder where Whittemore was sheltered. He knew just how many seconds the short fuses would take to reach the powder in the cans.

He struck a match, lit a fuse, counted. Rising up, he hurled the grenade.

It exploded before it hit. The blast boomed violently in the constricted space. The can was blown to bits, and the shock of it stunned the nest of rustlers, close to whom it went off.

One began crying out, wiping blood from his cut face.

The mustang with Pecos Carns on his back had stopped, fetlock deep in the creek water. The loud explosion had for a moment so startled the animal that his muscles were paralyzed. Then he snorted, reared high, turned and galloped back,

Carns bobbing up and down, slipping from the horse's back and dragging the ground.

Hatfield's second grenade sent three outlaws hastily scuttling from a rock nest to the left. One lay still behind them. He had received the full blast. Confusion, discouragement, were upon the rustlers. They had looked on their dead chief, they were short of ammunition, and the grenades finished it.

As the tall Ranger hurled a third one, a dozen rustlers left their hiding places and scurried toward the Pecos, shooting back as they ran.

"Come on, boys," called Hatfield. "We'll give 'em a run."

They cleared the canyon. Hatfield, before turning the corner, tossed a grenade to make sure the point was clear. Sand, smoke, bits of metal filled the air. Someone screamed, and the defenders charged the bend, reaching the Pecos.

Across the stream they saw some of the rustlers climbing out of the river canyon. They were a hundred yards upstream, and there was a steep but negotiable footpath at the point, partially hidden from the creek mouth by a bulge of the banks. Others were splashing in the Pecos, slipping on the rocks, as they sought to escape.

Still others were running up the bank to the point where they could cross to the trail.

"That's the way the squaw got out," thought Hatfield.

Whittemore and his men were crowding up to join the Ranger. They had clear beads on the outlaws, and opened fire. A rustler almost to the top of the canyon was hit, and crashed down, rolling and bouncing. He carried another outlaw with him.

"Throw down, rustlers!" bellowed Hatfield.

The Pecos rattled over the rock slide, the rapids purling white in the new daylight. Panic-stricken gunnies, realizing they could be picked off at will as they tried to climb to the top of the river canyon, began throwing down their weapons and raising their hands. Several near at hand called for mercy.

"Pick 'em up, Whittemore," ordered Hatfield. "Tie 'em and hold 'em."

He hurried back along the creek path. John Fenton and eight other ranchers were at the pass, lying in the rocks.

"Fenton!" called the Ranger.

"Hatfield!" shouted Fenton.

A blast of buckshot, sent by a hidden foe, whooshed past the towering bluff. But there weren't many enemies at the pass. The main bunch had been at the other end of the gorge, seeking to break through by way of the Pecos canyon.

"Carns is buzzard bait, rustlers!" called Hatfield, crouched just back of the turn. "Here's a present from the Rangers for yuh!"

He threw out a lighted grenade. The explosion banged in the ravine, and shrieks of hate and fear rose from enemy throats. He lit his last one, tossed it, and after it had gone off, he dashed around the turn, followed by John Fenton and the other ranchers.

The enemy ran for saddled horses up the line. The grenades had shocked them, sent them reeling back in dismay, and they sought only escape now. But Ranger lead, and the fire from the triumphant, cheering ranchers stopped them. Only two reached the mustangs and managed to ride off. The others quit, cowering with raised hands as the Ranger and Fenton ran up.

When the smoke of battle cleared, they took stock of the situation. Whittemore and Fenton had thirty prisoners. All knew now that Carns was finished, that their band was smashed. The handful who had been with Carns when he had died had fled, probably to Fentonville.

At the house, Emily Tate and Mrs. Fenton came toward Hatfield. There was anxious, beseeching light in their eyes. John Fenton, too, wanted to know about his son.

"Nat's got a good chance, folks," Hatfield told them. "He's in mighty fine hands in El Paso, and Jack's with him."

That was all he dared say at the moment. He wasn't yet sure of the outcome of the delicate operation.

"What next, Ranger?" asked Fred Whittemore. "Can we go back to our homes, now we've busted them rustlers?"

"I reckon. But first we better go clean up Fentonville. There's still a dozen or so of Carns' gang ain't seen the light yet. Fenton, we'll leave the folks under guard here and head for the settlement. Fetch along plenty of ammunition. . . ."

It was afternoon when they sighted the little town, with the blackened ruins of Barstowe's office building at the south end. Fentonville looked deserted in the heat. But as they rode rapidly in, several men ran out of the saloon and, jumping on mustangs, spurted away.

"That's what's left of the bunch," remarked Hatfield to Fenton. "I s'pose the ones who got away warned 'em."

"We can handle 'em, if they show their noses in these parts agin," growled Fenton.

There were some innocent bystanders in the settlement — inhabitants, and victims from whom Silas Barstowe had taken money in exchange for surrounding properties. Some of the investors had gone back to their homes to make ready to move, while others were out visiting the places they believed they had purchased.

"I'm goin' to entrust this money to you, Fenton," said Hatfield. "It belongs to the folks Barstowe's swindled. I hope to come up with Barstowe hisself and save the rest of it so it can be returned."

Chapter XIX

Clean-up

Silas Barstowe was not in Fentonville. He had left the night before and, with an escort of outlaws, had ridden south, perhaps to catch the morning train.

Hatfield took care of Goldy — he had picked up the sorrel on the way out of the hide-out — and enjoyed a hot meal and rest in town.

He took his leave of his friends then, and rode directly for the railroad, on Silas Barstowe's trail.

He reached the little station near the tracks after dark. There was a light burning in the shack of the agent, who informed him that Barstowe had caught the morning train for El Paso.

The Ranger was in time to signal an express, due in half an hour. The red lantern was hoisted to the pole by the track, and Hatfield waited till the searchlight pierced the night and the train roared in, grinding brakes squealing.

The conductor, seeing the Ranger star, nodded and grinned. He pulled the cord, and the train moved on.

It was the small hours of the morning when Hatfield left the train at the El Paso station. He had started through to the street when a man emerged from behind a half-closed door and hailed him.

"Ranger!"

It was Marshal Jack Greggs.

"Howdy, Greggs. So yuh've been keepin' watch like I asked yuh to!"

"Yes, suh! Day and night me or one of my deputies have been coverin' this station, watchin' for that Barstowe skunk. He come in yestiddy noon."

"Yuh didn't arrest him?"

"Nope. I done like yuh told me and had him follered. He's been havin' a party that's still goin' on — or was, half an hour ago when one of the boys reported to me. I was here, hopin' you'd come along."

"Good work, Marshal. The Rangers'll be mighty grateful for yore fine work."

Greggs was pleased, for he earnestly desired to atone for the error he had made in arresting Hatfield.

The long legs of the Texas Ranger moved rapidly, with Greggs trotting beside him as they moved up the wide street, blazing with lights. El Paso put on an all-night show. The party which Barstowe was giving was in a large private dining room at the back of the most ornate gambling palace in town.

Greggs had deputies covering the avenues of escape from the place. Hatfield, trailed by the marshal, walked through the main bar that was filled with merrymakers. Great batteries of oil lamps in crystal chandeliers heated the interior. Music filled the air and mingling with it were the shouts of drunks.

"Down that hall to the right," said Greggs. "Look out — there's one of his strong-arm men watchin' the corridor."

Hatfield swung along the hall. A waiter with a loaded tray pushed past him. A man in black, one of the fellows he had seen at Barstowe's El Paso offices, suddenly spied the tall officer — and he also spied the Colt which Hatfield threw into his slim hand.

The guard's mouth opened to speak, but then he thought better of it. Turning, he quickly glided away, leaving the door clear.

Hatfield opened it, looked in. The party had been going on for hours. Remains of chicken, lobsters, and other delicacies stood on the big round table. Champagne empties, other wine bottles, cigars, flowers, showed how well the banker's guests had dined. There were twenty, half of them gaudily dressed women. Several had gone to sleep on the carpet, but the survivors still sat at the circular table, drinking.

Barstowe's back was to the wall, so that he could have an eye on the door, but at the moment he had turned his head and Hatfield heard a drunken fellow, standing at the table, giving a toast to the host:

"Here's to good ol' Barstowe — here's to say g'by!"

"Leaving in the morning," Barstowe nodded. He clutched a burning cheroot, and he had drunk enough brandy to mellow him. "Hate to part, folks — good friends here. Goin' to Mexico, though, then Buenos Aires — cussed Ranger's fault."

Barstowe saw the tall officer who stood before him then, and his eyes flamed in alarm. His hands clawed, as he stared at Hatfield, whom he had believed was still at Fentonville.

Some of Carns' men had ridden to the town and told how Pecos Carns had died, and they had said that the Ranger had disappeared into the chaparral northwest of the settlement. Barstowe, believing he had reached El Paso unseen, had thought he had plenty of time to cross the Rio Grande and make good his escape.

"Stand up, and walk out ahead of me, Barstowe," ordered Hatfield quietly. "We don't want to hurt any of these ladies."

A cold silence came upon the guests. Men gulped, seeing the Ranger's star, pinned to the mighty Hatfield's coat. Greggs stood alert in the doorway.

Barstowe got up, a plump, bejeweled hand on the back of his gilt chair. He put down his cheroot, carefully, on his plate.

"Very well, sir," he said gruffly. "I will go with you. I have nothing to fear. I trust I may consult my lawyers?"

"Yuh may, if yuh figger it'll do yuh any good," drawled Hatfield.

"I've done nothing wrong," said Barstowe in a dignified voice, drawing himself up. "You have persecuted me, sir. My attorneys will rescue me from this stupid predicament. In a court of law, proof is required to convict a man."

Marshal Greggs snickered. "Listen, Barstowe! If yuh could hear Nat Fenton talkin', from his hospital bed, tellin' how yuh throwed in with Pecos Carns and his gang of killers, and all about the pizen yuh spiked yore victims' drinks with, yuh wouldn't want any more proof! He's gainin' strength and he'll be out in plenty time to testify agin yuh at yore trial. Won't be no bail for yuh, either. Yuh'll be held on killin' charges."

Barstowe was startled. He had believed that Nat Fenton, the most powerful witness to his perfidy and crimes, was insane, or dead.

It sent panic streaking through him, and his eyes blazed. He had the look of a cornered rat, and Hatfield knew he was going to fight, to try to break his way to freedom.

Barstowe's hand was quick, thrusting into the pocket of his coat. He did not draw the gun but fired through the cloth, his teeth gritted, his face burning red with his fury at Hatfield, who had tracked him down.

Hatfield felt the bite of the .32-caliber bullet, as it touched the skin of his left arm. His own shot, blaring from the big Colt caught Barstowe under the heart. The man staggered. He put his hand to his throat and his head flew back, as he gasped.

A girl screamed shrilly as Silas Barstowe fell heavily to the red velvet carpet, and from the front of the saloon came the gay strains of the dance.

★ ★ ★

"And that's the way it went, Cap'n," finished Jim Hatfield, as he reported to Bill McDowell at the Ranger Chief's Austin headquarters.

"Barstowe chose to die rather than dance at the end of a rope, huh!" said Captain Bill. "Good. Saves the State plenty of money."

"John Fenton's returnin' the cash I recovered from Carns and Barstowe, to the buyers. Young Nat's home by this time. That skull operation was successful and he's hisself agin. Him and that purty Em Tate'll hitch up, I reckon."

"Bueno. Glad you got it straightened out, Hatfield. Fenton and his friends worked hard for their range and they deserve to keep it. I hate to see folks put upon by slickers like that Barstowe, and by outlaws like Pecos Carns."

"Yuh may have a couple recruits, Cap'n, next year. Barney Porter and his friends are likin' the Rangers mighty well."

"I don't wonder at that. They seen you workin', and that's enough to excite any boy. If they measure up, I may give 'em a chance at that."

McDowell frowned, reached over, picked up a sheaf of reports from his wire basket.

"There's always plenty to do in Texas," he remarked, rattling the papers. "I could use more Rangers. I hate to work the few I got so hard."

Hatfield grinned, held out his hand.

"Let me have 'em, Cap'n. Workin' rests me and Goldy."

"Well, it's a big fuss on the Nueces this time . . . But I ain't s'posed to git excited." McDowell cleared his throat. He began to count, "One — two — three — four!" He paused to explain, "Doc says if I count to ten 'fore I blow off I'll . . . shucks!"

The gnarled fist hit the desk, the inkwell jumped, and sulphurous language issued from McDowell.

Soon, Captain Bill stood in the sunshine of the open window. He watched Jim Hatfield mount the golden sorrel, to carry the law to the new point of danger, to protect the mighty reaches of the Lone Star State.

WILLENHALL

235

We hope you have enjoyed this Large Print book. Other Thorndike, Wheeler or Chivers Press Large Print books are available at your library or directly from the publishers.

For more information about current and upcoming titles, please call or write, without obligation, to:

Publisher
Thorndike Press
295 Kennedy Memorial Drive
Waterville, ME 04901
Tel. (800) 223-1244

Or visit our Web site at:
www.gale.com/thorndike
www.gale.com/wheeler

OR

Chivers Large Print
published by BBC Audiobooks Ltd
St James House, The Square
Lower Bristol Road
Bath BA2 3BH
England
Tel. +44(0) 800 136919
email: bbcaudiobooks@bbc.co.uk
www.bbcaudiobooks.co.uk

All our Large Print titles are designed for easy reading, and all our books are made to last.